TWISTED DEVIL

VICIOUS VIPERS MC 4

LYNN BURKE

Copyright © 2020 by Lynn Burke

All rights reserved.

Editor: Avril Stepowski

Cover Design by Golden Czermak/FuriousFotog

This is a work of fiction. Names, characters, places, and incidents are the product of the author's imagination or are used fictitiously, and any resemblance to actual persons, living or dead, business establishments, events, or locales is entirely coincidental.

No part of this book may be reproduced in any form, except for the inclusion of brief quotations in a review or article, without written permission from the author.

Visit my website at authorlynnburke.com

TWISTED DEVIL

Hacking is my specialty, extortion my means of keeping the Vicious Vipers MC in the money. I'm a devil who thrives on forcing sinners to atone for their corrupt ways since the one who damaged my soul escaped punishment.

When a battered, too-young woman shows up at our club searching for sanctuary, finding a way through her walls becomes my obsession. She ties my stomach in knots—and I know she'll be the key to unravelling them.

My plan to possess her abides by the law, but my thirst for her torments my restraint. I'll risk it all to show her she has worth, to claim her as my property.

She believes she's tainted. Stained.

I'll move heaven and hell to make her see we can be beautifully broken—together.

DEDICATION

For Cindy & Kelly K.

CONTENTS

1. Dasia — 1
2. Devil — 12
3. Dasia — 26
4. Devil — 37
5. Dasia — 44
6. Devil — 54
7. Dasia — 62
8. Devil — 74
9. Dasia — 80
10. Devil — 87
11. Dasia — 94
12. Devil — 99
13. Dasia — 108
14. Devil — 116
15. Dasia — 134
16. Devil — 146
17. Dasia — 158
18. Devil — 165
19. Dasia — 169
20. Devil — 177
21. Dasia — 186
22. Devil — 194
23. Dasia — 200
24. Devil — 212
25. Dasia — 216
26. Devil — 224
27. Dasia — 231
28. Devil — 238

About the Author 244
Also By Lynn Burke 245

I jolted awake with a gasp, the memory of rope around my wrists and ankles biting my tender flesh still lingering as I took in the dimly lit bedroom around me.

Soft mattress, I told myself as my heart thrummed with enough force to power the Infinity Gauntlet. *Clean sheets that smell like a spring day.*

A double guest bed with its pink fluffy comforter, a chest of drawers, and one bed stand stuffed into the small guest room along with me, and I was safe.

For now.

Sucking in oxygen, I forced myself to relax by focusing on filling my lungs and slowly emptying them. I had escaped my captors three days earlier and found refuge with my old case worker, Pia, and her badass biker boyfriend, Ryker.

At seventeen, I was still a ward of the state and should have been tossed back into another foster home, but Pia had promised me the night before she would do no such thing. I'd been in one shitty home after another for which she had always apologized for, begging me to hang in there until she could find me something better.

My final foster father had creeped me the hell out from day one, and he ended up being the thief of my innocence I'd been saving. I'd hoped to find that one man someday, my knight in shining armor fate had waiting for me.

Curling in on myself, arms around my knees, I fought against the despair that any good man would want someone broken by rape. My throat tightened, but I refused to allow that man to do more damage than he already had.

I'd run away even as the asshole had begged forgiveness for his demons. The sick fuck. Rather than run to my social worker, Miss Pia, I'd taken to the streets, dancing at some seedy joint in South Boston for fists full of dollars seven nights a week.

That's where Ivan had found me. If that was even his real name.

Sexy Russian accent and super sweet, like a boy next door wanting nothing but my company, he knew how to weasel his way past my walls, using all those words a hurting soul needs to hear.

He'd turned out to be an asshole, too.

I closed my eyes against the morning sunlight peeking around the blinds with their lacey valances and let out a heavy exhale, trying to calm myself. Ridding my mind of what I'd been through in the previous few months would take some doing. And time. I held onto that hope like a piece of driftwood while bobbing up and down in the sea of life. A few weeks from becoming an adult in the state's sight, and I floundered already.

Lost. Alone in my pain, my fears.

Miss Pia had asked dozens of questions before telling me to get some rest, but I hadn't shared half of what had transpired since I'd last seen her weeks earlier. She felt guilty for my predicament, claiming if she'd taken me out of the Griffey's home the first time I told her about his wandering hands...

I refused to hear it, though. Miss Pia had never been anything but kind, motherly in a way none of my foster mothers had ever been. The pain on her face while tucking me in had set a heaviness in my chest. I'd never been as cared for. Never felt so looked after.

Perhaps I didn't have to be alone after all. Maybe she and her scary biker boyfriend would let me stay until my birthday.

Grasping desperately at that idea and breathing deeply, I noted the scents of cinnamon and bacon—and coffee.

I popped my eyelids open again as my stomach made its protest from the lack of food the previous week or so. Pia had fed me after I'd showered the night before, but the sandwich hadn't begun to fill the void inside my stomach.

A soft knock sounded, jerking my focus toward the door.

I grasped the comforter beneath my chin. "Yeah?"

"It's me, Dasia."

A rush of air escaped me at Miss Pia's voice. "Come on in."

I relaxed my hold on the blanket as she came in, a steaming mug in her hand.

"Still like your coffee with extra cream and sugar?"

An ache spread up my throat at her remembering, and I nodded while sitting to prop against the headboard. "Thanks," I managed to rasp as she handed the mug to me and sat on the bed's edge. I hadn't had my morning coffee for close to two weeks.

"How'd you sleep?"

"Like a rock—until a messed up early morning nightmare." Frowning, I sipped the coffee, and my brow eased at the perfection of the sugary deliciousness burning its way straight to my stomach. "So good."

"Want to talk about it?"

I sipped again, the scalding heat a welcome distraction from the images still flashing through my head. I'd told Miss Pia some of what had happened —more the *what*, not the details that were enough to churn my guts half to death. *Did* I want to talk about it?

"Not really," I finally answered her, "but maybe spewing out all the shit of the last two weeks or so would be good, huh?" God knows I'd spent enough time with therapists over the years to know getting the words past tight lips helped out a bit.

"I think it would." Her kind smile—and the good night's rest—made spilling easier, and once I started from the point of the rape and running away, the story spewed from my lips without hesitation, fear she might be disgusted by my bad choices, without embarrassment those choices had led me to hell.

Ivan had talked me into going out for coffee one night after work—and he clocked me upside the head before we even pulled out of the parking lot. I'd woken, bound and gagged in a basement-like room with no windows.

Cold and alone. Scared shitless and hungry as hell.

My clothes had been askew when I came to—no panties beneath my skirt—but no sting, no blood, no throbbing ache between my thighs lingered like when my foster father had taken what didn't belong to him.

Attacking Ivan, once let free of my restraints, that first day in my prison had only landed me on my ass, head ringing, and body bruised. Coldness had replaced his flirty, suave smile. A frigid demeanor ruled his face, and silenced his vocal cords. I'd asked —screamed—a thousand and one questions, begging for answers whenever he visited with a daily tray of food, but he refused to speak a word to me.

At least he'd provided a bucket and toilet paper. But after a few days, with nothing but a dirty floor to sleep on and no other amenities to speak of, my hopes of ever seeing the light of day faded.

What seemed like years later, even though I'd counted ten daily food trays, I once more found myself bound with biting ropes, a pillowcase over my head, and carried up a flight of stairs by Ivan and two men I'd never seen before that day. They grunted to each other in Russian, before tossing me into a vehicle, none-too gently. Ages had passed before the forward motion stopped. Cool air licked at my feverish skin as snot and tears dirtied my already filthy face beneath the pillow case taped tight around my neck.

I was a nobody, worthless even to whomever had spawned my ass, so I knew my kidnapping had nothing to do with a ransom.

My fears over a future I couldn't control became known for sure when Ivan and his two buddies locked me up in a metal container, one where twenty other young women huddled together against the far end.

Sex slavery, I told Miss Pia. I'd had no doubt.

A life of submission and servitude—and probably physical abuse beyond the sexual I would be powerless to stop once sold. But we hadn't been sold within that first hour or so, and I'd decided I would escape—or die trying.

For two days, we weren't fed or let out to use a

bathroom. Thirst set in to combat our mind's obsession with fear, but I held onto my sanity as others whimpered and cried, their hope already gone before I'd even arrived.

I refused to accept my reality—and I talked all but two of the oldest women to go berserk once the door opened again. While I certainly wasn't a born leader, someone had needed to step up to the plate if we wanted to fight for our future. Three strong men appeared in the light spilling through the door, but we out-numbered them by seventeen. Surely, a bunch of wild, eye-ball scratching, biting, and screaming women stood a chance.

"I'm not sure how many of us actually made it off the docks," I whispered to Miss Pia, the girls' screams still in my ears. "There were two other men beyond those three—and only a handful of other girls even made it outside the container."

"Where were you?"

"Down near the harbor—I doubt I would even remember if I saw the place again. I was so freaked out, so desperate, I managed to focus on one hiding spot after another, once even jumping into the water to escape them."

Face pale, Miss Pia studied me with a stare that had always rooted out my thoughts and feelings.

"Would you be able to pick Ivan out of a group of men?"

I nodded without hesitation. "Definitely."

"And the others?"

I shrugged, tightening my grip on the empty mug still clasped in my hands. "Not sure—probably not."

Miss Pia let out a heavy exhale and patted my knee through the comforter. "I'm not going to inform my old boss that you're here, Dasia. You'll be eighteen in less than three weeks. This room is yours for as long as you want."

Tears sprang to my eyes, and I found myself slumping against the headboard, not having realized my entire body had tensed tight from my tale. "Seriously?"

Lips in a thin line, she nodded. "While it's not right in the eyes of the law, I'm coming to not care about that fact as much as I used to."

I swiped the back of my hand over my cheek to stop the leaking tears as I considered the scowling biker who owned the house we sat in—and probably the influence behind her change of heart. I'll admit to being slightly spooked by the dude. "Isn't this Ryker's place? What does he think about my staying?"

The severity of her face eased up a bit, a small

smile lighting her blue-green eyes. "He'll do what-ever I want because he loves me."

Damn. My throat tightened up again. *To be loved like that. Number one in someone's life...*

"I've got baked French toast in the oven and he's making bacon," Miss Pia said, patting my knee again. "Why don't you come down and have some breakfast with us? You'll need to tell Ryker the jist of what happened, so we can decide on what to do next."

"Got any more of this coffee? It's wicked good."

She laughed lightly while standing. "Plenty of it. Take your time, though. No rush."

Once she shut the bedroom door softly behind her, I eyed the leggings and sweatshirt she'd given me the night before, folded at the foot of the bed. I grabbed the leggings and pulled them on, but paused while considering the sweatshirt.

The zippered hoodie Ryker's friend had given me the night before—Devil, both Pia and Ryker had called him—lay atop the chest of drawers. I padded over the cool hardwood flooring and snatched it up, lifting it to my nose.

The sweet scent of licorice and an underlying musk of absolute deliciousness flooded my senses.

Damn.

I sniffed again, remembering his firm yet tender grip on my arms after he'd told me to put it on the night before as I'd stood shivering outside the Vicious Vipers' club. He had a raspy, sexy as hell voice, enough so that just the memory of the low timbre sent tingles throughout my entire body.

Frowning, I reminded myself men couldn't be trusted, I shoved my arms into the sleeves, zippering the too-big sweatshirt up to my chin like my own vibranium shield against the world.

Going through shit might break a person down, but in the movies, they usually rose from the ashes. While I wasn't anywhere near ready to sprout wings, I lifted my chin and strode out into the hallway like my shoulder blades tingled.

I'd managed to escape a life of sexual slavery, surely I would be able to face down my kidnappers some day and tell the tale that would get their asses locked up.

I might have been broken, but maybe someday, I would find what Miss Pia had—a happily ever after.

2
____

DEVIL

etween the memory of that curvy red-head's body, the pain in her eyes, and the unknown of the why she'd shown up at the club's gate looking like she'd been dragged behind a bike for a few miles and left for dead, I didn't sleep worth a shit.

Dasia Walker. Seventeen-year-old ward of the state. Too fucking young and too fucking hot for her own—and my own—good.

Over a month ago, I'd dug deep to get the scoop on the girl when Ryker had asked. I'd seen a few pictures, but the girl wasn't on social media at all. Not a goddamn single site to let me into her head. See who she was behind the pretty face and sad eyes.

Tons of women looked pretty in pictures, but seeing Dasia in the flesh that first time had my dick fucking rock hard with the need to claim before I even realized who the girl was.

The rush of adrenaline, the thirst for her, was more than mere lust. Everything about her—makeup-less face, bright red hair, tied my stomach up in fucking knots. I knew, too, she would be the key to unraveling them.

Instantaneous rage accompanied the hard-on from hell—someone had hurt her, and the need to kill the fucker had me tense from head to toe.

Didn't give a fuck she was only seventeen.

Didn't give a fuck I wasn't a mean mother-fucker like my brothers Ryker, Stone, or Vigil.

Didn't give a fuck my hands got more revenge through a laptop than with a fist or gripping a gun.

All I cared about was wrapping that girl up—and not with the ropes my kinky ass preferred. I wanted her protected. Revenged. Safe.

Knowing Ryker could easily provide that himself didn't keep me from grinding my teeth in frustration. I'd called him for answers five times the night before after he, Pia, and Dasia had driven off in his truck. Didn't get a goddamn peep out of him.

Nothing. Not even a goddamn text telling me she was okay.

I called at seven a.m. after waiting a solid two hours for his ass to wake up, not wanting to hear he needed a few cups of coffee before becoming human.

Fucking nothing other than a grunted reply that Dasia still slept.

I enclosed myself in the second bedroom of my small house I'd made into an office, the chair beneath me molding to my ass and back like a lover. We'd spent many hours—months—together, doing what I did best.

"Computer shit" as my brothers called it.

A brilliant mind wasted, one of my professors at MIT had declared when I told him I was dropping out.

Wasn't a waste when put to good use, though. Sneaking through backdoors and designing untraceable rootkits came easy as breathing for me. Somedays, I wondered if my brain was actually a government super computer of their own building. Created to infiltrate, manipulate, and destroy whatever fucking system it wanted—because it came *too* fucking easy even for my own comfort.

But that brain also proved nothing and nobody tracked me. There was no wall or dead end I couldn't break through or escape.

A silent thief in the night, a simple guy who'd been wronged and had taken it upon himself to bring sinners' misdeeds to light and make them pay.

It's what I did.

It's what earned me the nickname Devil with the Vicious Vipers MC.

It's what lined my pockets and theirs while bringing justice to those who thought themselves above the law.

Dasia Walker's face stared back at me from the many screens atop my semi-circular desk. Those sad, haunted eyes muddling my damn head. She'd been abused according to what Ryker had told me—and the fucker who'd raped her took his last breath weeks earlier.

I didn't have the details of how on that last part, but I'd seen Ryker in action. Ted Griffey hadn't met a pleasant end, that much I would bet my own life on.

Fucker deserved it, abusing a young woman like that.

My jaw ached as memories long buried in the back of my head tried to surface. It had been years since I'd thought about them, and shoving that shit back in the hell hole it snuck out of came a bit harder than usual. Having seen Dasia and knowing somewhat what she went through emotionally, fucking ripped my mind and heart in two.

No child, whether eleven or seventeen, deserved such treatment.

Dasia sure as fuck didn't look seventeen, though.

"Fuck." I rubbed a hand over the top of my head, messing up my too-long hair. Time for a fade and trim up top—but it could wait until I got answers.

I grabbed my silent cell off my desk, and the screen lit up before I could swipe to unlock it and bother Ryker again.

"Ryker. Fucking finally," I snipped when answering.

"Fuck off, you obsessive prick."

"How is she?"

"I'm calling Vigil for a meeting in an hour," he said, rather than answer me, his low tone pissed beyond the usual broodiness he usually portrayed through voice and facial tics.

"What happened?"

"I'm not getting into it over the phone. Just get your ass to the club."

The fucker hung up.

Cursing, I hopped up and did as told, black bag with my laptop over my shoulder.

———

I'd never been so livid in my life. My gut churned, filling me with the desire to slash throats and grin while watching blood spill down over my boots.

Ryker had told the Viper officers gathered in Vigil's office what Dasia had gone through the previous couple of weeks, and my fucking heart ached for the girl while my fingertips itched to rip flesh rather than tap keys.

She'd been tied up in a goddamn basement for days on end without a real toilet or running water. Tossed into a container with a bunch of other women, the darkness and cold, never mind the fear, giving them one last push to attempt freedom.

Sure, I found her beyond attractive, and my dick hadn't given up on the idea of erasing all thoughts of her rape from her mind, but the need to *protect* her simmered in my blood ... I felt like a goddamn animal driven by instincts.

"Devil!"

I jerked my head toward Ryker who still stood beside the office door, arms crossed and scowling.

"You listening?"

I wanted to clear my throat and shift like a kid caught with its hand in the candy bowl, but held his stare without flinching. "Yeah."

Ryker turned toward Vigil who sat behind his desk with a scowl deep as Ryker's denting his forehead. "She'll be staying at my place," Ryker continued.

"You going to notify social services?" Vigil asked.

"Fuck no. If Pia couldn't protect her, no one can."

Ryker had told me Pia tried countless times to find her a new foster home—and blamed herself for failing.

"She'll be eighteen in less than three weeks," Ryker continued. "The state isn't gonna find her here in that time, and why would they give a fuck anyway? One less life for them to worry about."

"Think the fuckers who took her are going to come looking for her, though?" Ricky, our VP and Vigil's brother, asked, his gaze flitting from one officer to the next. "She's seen too much," he said when no one answered.

"She's under our protection," Vigil stated, and I

sat just a bit easier having his word as law set firmly in place.

Ryker dipped his head in acknowledgement, his shoulders relaxing the slightest as well. "Thank you."

"Why don't you bring her down to the dojo?" Stone said from his spot on the couch where he leaned forward, elbows on his knees, his blue eyes intent as always. "I'll set her up with karate classes in the mornings—teach her how to really throw a kick to the ball sack."

She'd dropped one of the fuckers according to Ryker's retelling of Dasia's escape, but I leaped on Stone's idea.

"Fuck, yeah. Give her a sense of empowerment, too."

Ricky nodded in agreement of my words.

"Appreciate it, Stone," Ryker said. "When she's ready, I'll give you a holler. I'm going to make some calls to old buddies in Southie and see what shit I can stir up," he told Vigil. "She said they spoke Russian, so I'm thinking it could be connected to the fucker Arturo was working with out in Vegas."

I glanced over at Stone to see his face shut down, void of emotion. His woman, Giada, had been snagged and was being auctioned off when he,

Ryker, and Klingon, the president of the Vipers' Vegas chapter, had gone in, knives slashing and guns blazing to rescue her.

The bigwig Russian asshole had met his end—and so did Arturo, the head of the Martínez cartel at the time. Ryker had found out a few months earlier, Arturo's cousin—his childhood friend—had taken over the family business once they'd assumed Arturo had somehow met his end since he'd never returned to South America.

"Think Martínez is involved?" I asked about that friend, sitting back and crossing my arms to keep my fingers still when they burned to tap keys and start digging.

"Arrogant cocksucker," Ryker muttered. "Wouldn't surprise me. Martínez's threat to take care of shit if he found out we were involved in Arturo's disappearance still fucking hangs heavy over me, but Klingon assured me yesterday afternoon before this whole Dasia fiasco that all is quiet out there."

"How's Jenny?" I asked about his sister who had decided to travel out to Vegas to stay with a friend after her and Ryker's mom passed a couple months earlier.

"Talked to her last night. She says she's good— she's got no clue I've got Klingon covering her ass in case Martínez finds shit out and tries to exact revenge on us."

"It's been long enough, I'm thinking those Vegas Vipers know how to clean up messes."

Stone agreed with me, but Ricky merely grunted, the glass-half-empty fuck.

"Devil," Vigil said, drawing my attention back across the desk, "fire that laptop up and work your magic."

"Gladly."

"Find out what—who exactly, law and outlaw—we could be taking on if we decide to get involved."

"We're already involved, fucker," Ricky grumbled his favorite nickname for his big brother.

Vigil and our VP had a nice long stare down before Vigil finally turned away. "She's under our protection until she decides to leave. If we're right in our thinking this is part of a sex slave operation involving the Russian mafia and possibly the Martínez cartel, we can't take them on."

"We can if they don't know we're doing it," I tossed out.

Vigil turned his focus on me.

I shrugged, having complete confidence in my abilities to unearth shit and make people pay the devil for stupid ass choices. "Just a matter of time and effort. I'm sure I can find enough shit to take both organizations down if we really wanted to."

"The Russian mob is world-wide, asshole," Ricky muttered.

"And computers are, too, you miserable cock-sucker," I offered back with a grin. "Contrary to what you might think, if shit is tangible—hell, even if it's superstition—it's buried in a network somewhere for black hats like me to sneak in and find."

"Cocky fucker."

"I call it confidence—fucking *fact*."

"That's enough," Vigil grunted. "Devil, you get the evidence to clean up Boston at least, and it's a step in the right direction. Can you send that info to your contact at the FBI we unloaded the Burtonelli and Arturo shit to?"

I nodded, still grinning at Ricky who seriously needed to get laid, the grumpy fuck.

"Then do what you do best," Vigil said. "Find what we need to keep these fuckers away from Dasia and maybe help in taking down whatever fucking rings actually exist."

"Could always toss a bone to Burtonelli and get him involved," I suggested, glancing over at Stone. "Not that we owe him jack shit or that Giada is even interested in smoothing things over with her family, but with him leading in the polls and running for that seat on cleaning up our state..." I shrugged. "Might put him in our back pocket again."

A muscle ticked in Stone's jaw.

"Fuck him," Vigil said, ending Stone's deliberation. "Giada's sister told her their father hasn't breathed a word about the Vipers since that shit show ended, and I have no wish to stir up that fucking pot again."

"And if he gets elected like the polls are almost guaranteeing and he comes screaming for the outlaw bikers who enticed his daughter away?" Ricky the downer just had to ask while glancing between Vigil and Stone.

"Then all the shit I have on him will go public, just like we promised," I jumped in before the brothers started up and someone bloodied a nose.

"He's nothing to worry about right now, anyway," Vigil said, waving his hand like a black fly buzzed past his face, putting an end to the Burtonelli topic.

A few more club details, and he told us to get the fuck out and get shit done.

Ryker pinned me with a glare, and his tip of the head indicating I follow him had me on his heels as we stepped outside into the Indian summer morning.

"What do you want with the girl?" he asked, striding toward our bikes.

Loaded fucking question, right there. I wanted *her*. Tied to my bed. At my mercy. Under me. In my goddamn head—but would she let me have her after what those pricks had done to her?

"You keep your paws off her," he said, when I didn't answer.

I decided to keep my thoughts to myself and give him the tamer response. "What I want is to protect her—make things right."

He climbed on his bike and lifted an eyebrow my way while firing up his Screamin Eagle. "She's off limits, Devil—and I fucking mean it. I saw the way you looked at her, and you're the last fucker she needs sniffing after her ass, got it?"

I nodded to let him know I'd heard. "Cool your jets, daddy-o. I'm going home to dig up all the shit I can to make the fuckers pay."

Lips pressed in a tight line, he revved the engine and took off through the compound's gate that hadn't yet fully squeaked open on its rollers.

I hopped onto my old CVO Street Glide—my beautiful orange baby—and followed, my mind set on what I had to do in order to end the fuckers who'd hurt my woman, because she was just that.

My woman. Zero fucking doubt.

I just had to get her to stick around long enough to give me a shot in helping her learn to trust humans with dicks again—and cool Ryker's jets so I could *bury* my face in that ass, not just sniff after it.

3

DASIA

For a girl who'd enjoyed dancing on stage and stripping out of my clothes for cash, I hung at the back of the dojo, wishing to be a wallflower. Ryker's friend, Stone, owned the place and had offered classes to help me learn some self-defense.

Just in case Ivan and his Russian buddies came looking for the birdie who'd escaped their cage.

I hadn't thought much about that fact until Ryker had brought it up over breakfast a few days earlier. He'd assured me that the Vipers would keep me safe with such confidence and a gleam in his cold greenish eyes that a shiver had slid down my spine.

Immediately, my mind had gone to my foster father who'd gotten mugged and hours later begged forgiveness for touching me that first time. Then my mind went to his disappearance after the rape.

I didn't ask, though. Didn't want to know anything that would incriminate Pia's man.

If Ryker and his friends, or brothers as he called them, considered themselves above the law and took matters into their own hands, it would be best to stay in the dark and not be able to have truth pried from my lips.

Loyal friends but terrifying enemies. Just like the mafia and the movies I adored depicting that kind of family life. It felt good to be somewhat on the inside, but it felt even better knowing they had my six, as Ryker called it.

Still, I remained quiet at the back of the class so as not to draw attention to myself, learning to chamber my leg before snapping it out in front of my body. I studied the handful of other adult students in front of me, shifting my stance and pivoting as they did, my kicks and punches not nearly as fast as theirs.

While I'd built back up some of my energy that the weeks in captivity had depleted, I struggled to keep from getting too winded.

Sensei Jason, Stone's dojo manager and class teacher, wasn't a Viper brother, but they'd known one another for over fifteen years. If he had Stone, and thus Ryker's trust, he had mine.

At the end of the forty-five minute class, I had sweated through the t-shirt beneath the gi Stone had given me. Pia smiled from the chairs alongside the mats when I finally exhaled in relief at being done and turned to find her gaze on me.

"You did so well!" she said with a big smile as I collapsed onto the chair beside her, grabbing at the bottle of water she'd suggested I bring along.

"I'm *so* out of shape."

She huffed a snort. "Hardly. Karate is tough—I'm proud of you for even sticking through to the end of the class. I know I wouldn't."

I swallowed a gulp of water, and it eased the thickness her words had brought. No one had ever told me they were proud of me. "Thanks," I whispered, capping the water again.

Ten minutes later, we pulled into Ryker's driveway, and I stood beneath the shower's spray for half of forever, still feeling as though the stench and dirt of that basement clung to my skin.

At least tears didn't pour down my cheeks as they'd done that first night Pia had offered me the use of their bathroom.

Only three days, but emotionally, I'd made a lot of progress as far as I was concerned. I'll admit to growing bored, though. The three of us had gone shopping that first afternoon, much to Ryker's annoyance, but he refused to let us go off alone while buying me clothes, shoes, and other necessities. I'd told Pia to keep track and I promised to pay her back as soon as I could.

The following two days I had rested and watched a shit ton of movies—the Marvel heroes from beginning to end, my favorites of all times.

I'd been thrilled to learn about the dojo class and even more excited to start. I expected, though, my body wouldn't be too happy with me the next morning.

Talk about jelly legs. I had to hang onto the shower door while climbing out of the stall, but at least I found myself grinning over the fact rather than hating it. Ryker had signed me up for three morning classes every week, and I expected I would appreciate that day off in between.

"How was the class?" Ryker asked when I joined them for dinner that evening.

"Awesome. I'm gonna feel it tomorrow, though."

"Anyone make you feel uncomfortable? Checking you out or shit like that?"

I bit back a smirk at his pissy tone and shook my head.

"Good," he grunted as Pia dished up the American chop suey she'd made. "Any of those fuckers so much as looks at you the wrong way, you tell me, Stone, or Sensei Jason if we're not around."

I nodded and dug in, rich tomato sauce and tender hamburger with al dente elbow noodles quickly filling my stomach.

"Certainly worked up an appetite," Pia said, a smile in her voice.

I peered up at her, realizing I hovered over my bowl like a starving animal. "Sorry."

Really, I had no rush to eat since a few hours of nothingness sat ahead of me until I crashed, and another full day of similar nothing to wake up to.

Pia and I had already discussed me getting my GED, but she suggested holding off a bit to keep me out of the system until any fall out from my escape disappeared.

I hated school and had gladly agreed. But, I needed something to do.

"I need a job," I blurted out, thinking about the clothes on my back and the slippers on my feet that they'd bought for me.

"Not happening," Ryker said, the grump.

Frowning, I stared at him as he shoveled another mouthful of dinner between his lips. He must have felt my unwavering attention, because he lifted his gaze to me, an eyebrow quirked.

"I need to pay you back," I said, holding up my index finger, "and two, I'm going to go bat shit crazy sitting here every day all day until it's safe for me to head off on my own. Not that I'm complaining," I hastened to add. "I'm wicked appreciative of all you've given me."

Ryker chewed and studied me until I shifted my attention back on the little bit of food left in my bowl. "I could use some help at the shop."

Pia made a noise under her breath, one I couldn't figure out the meaning of, but glancing between the two had me wishing I had someone I knew well enough to communicate silently with. No one would want to know my broken soul that well, though. Tainted. Stained. Used.

And anyway, the thought of allowing a man that far inside my head, let alone my body, turned my insides squeamish.

A longing for, yet repulsion by any type of intimacy with a man, swirled in my stomach.

The man who gave me the sweatshirt, though, he didn't turn my stomach. I took to sleeping with that piece of clothing, the fading scent of licorice more a soothing balm than turn on.

"She's a part of this family now," Ryker finally said, and my mind jerked from hot biker guy to tears in a heartbeat.

Part of their family... My throat tightened.

Pia eyed him in silence a few moments longer. "If she works at the shop, she'll know Viper business."

Ryker turned toward me while chewing another bite, his cold gaze not bothering me as much as it used to as he seemed to peer inside me like Pia did. "There's a party at the club this weekend. Want to go?"

We'd be surrounded by big, bad bikers, beer, and loud music—probably. Ryker's brothers I trusted with my life since he'd said their president put me under their protection. Did I want to see the rest of the family he claimed I belonged to ... and Devil, the hot one I couldn't get out of my head, especially while laying in bed at night?

"Hell, yeah," I said, unable to keep from grinning.

Ryker nodded. "The shop's office is a hell hole, just warning you," he muttered, going back to our earlier conversation, "but I'll pay you cash under the table."

"I want you to withhold money every week until I pay you back for the clothes and stuff," I said, snagging another eyebrow raise.

"Sure thing, little birdie," he said. "If that's what you want."

My smile widened as he stuck his hand out across the table. His calloused hand gripped mine as we agreed old-school style.

I had a job—and a biker party to look forward to.

———

Saturday late afternoon, we drove in Ryker's truck over to the club, the potato salad and brownies Pia and I had made as our contributions to the cookout on the back seat beside me.

Although late September, an Indian summer lingered, leaving me free to wear short sleeves with my skinny jeans. Flip flops were out for the season, unfortunately, so I opted for the Harley boots Ryker insisted I would need as part of the Viper family.

Excitement churned my stomach in a good way, and my palms sweated while gripping the plate of brownies, but I couldn't keep from smiling as we walked behind the club and across the compound to a large grassy area.

Smoke from two huge grills wafted by on the warm breeze, making my mouth water. Music blasted from a kickass Bose system, and although no drunk chicks danced—yet—a dozen or so little kids ran around screaming, playing what appeared to be tag.

That, I hadn't expected, even though I expected some of the Vipers must be married with spawn. The Vipers weren't just an outlaw club, they were real families with kids and dogs even, drinking lemonade and eating burgers and dogs like a normal Fourth of July party.

A tingle raced up my spine, raising the hairs on my neck as I set the brownies on the dessert table a woman named Shaun had pointed to when Pia asked where we ought to put the food. I glanced over my shoulder while wiping my still damp palms down my jeans.

Licorice man, Devil, stood with a few other men on the other end of the green. I felt his stare over the distance, even with people flitting through our line of vision. He had the type of heavy-hooded bedroom eyes women swooned over, amber brown and fathomless, the type that affected me in all the right—or wrong—places whether I wanted them to or not.

Ryker approached the group, and Devil ripped

his focus off me, allowing me to draw air I hadn't realized I'd withheld from my lungs.

That man dampened my panties with a mere meeting of our eyes, and my brow furrowed even as my heart raced, wishing for more of that connection. The look he'd given me combated with the memory of his gentle touch that night I'd shown up at the Vipers' club.

I glanced over to find his focus glued to me once more. He watched me with unnerving intensity, like he wanted to tie me up and have his wicked way with me, age be damned. Rather than be freaked out as I should have been, all sorts of delicious shivers pebbled my skin at the thought of being bound and at his mercy.

Sick.

I cursed the fresh rush of dampness between my thighs.

I'm sick. Broken by that damn kidnapping and by Mr. Griffey.

Clenching my jaw, I turned away, ambling toward where Pia still spoke with Shaun. I tried to focus on pleasantries, doing adult-like shit, but couldn't keep from glancing at Devil, covertly checking him out when he wasn't facing me.

He knew how to wear a pair of jeans, snug to his

ass rather than hanging off his hips like guys my age. I also liked the navy t-shirt stretched over his broad shoulders and tucked into his trim waist.

He wasn't a hulk of a man like some of the other Vipers—especially the beast-like man on his opposite side from Ryker, but I appreciated his leaner physique. Ripped forearms veined and sexy as hell as he clutched a bottle of beer had my fingers wanting to explore.

I knew that night in bed I'd be thinking about those arms, those hands, while hugging his sweatshirt against my front, wishing I could still breathe in the scent of licorice and warmth.

That warmth lingered deep inside me, making me needy in a way I'd never known before. Butterflies erupted inside me when he turned his attention on me while Ryker spoke to him.

Caught drooling, I quickly turned away, that damn war of want and aversion going at it inside my head and heart.

Sick.

4

DEVIL

"So far it's shaping up to be way more than we can handle on our own," I told Vigil, Ryker, and the other officers standing with me, the cold brew in my hand almost as distracting as Dasia standing on the other side of the lawn. "Too big an operation, too many crooked fingers in the pot."

"Figured it would be," Ricky muttered with his usual downer tone while the others stayed quiet.

"I'm going to keep digging," I continued, fighting to keep my focus on Vigil rather than the gorgeous red-head across the lawn. "Pile up a shitload of evidence the FBI can't seem to find on their own. It's out there. I just got to find it all, make sure not a single fucker in the sex slave trade here in New England escapes unnoticed."

"We're definitely out of this one," he said. 'We've got too many old ladies and children around here that need protecting."

Ryker grumbled something under his breath, catching Vigil's glare as though he'd heard the words I hadn't.

"I know it's personal for you, having taken Dasia in," Vigil told him, "but this time, we're gonna have to let the law take it into their own hands."

"I'd like to go after that Ivan fucker," Ryker said, glancing toward where I could feel Dasia's stare.

"Right there with ya," I agreed and swigged my beer.

Ryker glanced at me. "She's in my house," he snipped. "My care. Under my protection. Might as well be my own fucking kid. If she wasn't going to be eighteen in a couple of weeks, Pia would probably have us adopting her ass. She doesn't need or want any sexual advances from a twisted fuck like you. Keep your goddamn paws off."

"Yeah, I heard you the first time."

We stared at one another while I swigged again, and tension rose from the brothers with us.

"The fuck is going on?" Vigil asked.

"Daddy-o here, thinks I'm going to talk Dasia into a little kink. Tie her up and fuck her ass raw."

Ryker's glare turned murderous, his shoulders hitching higher, but I knew he wouldn't come after me with all the brothers around.

"See, thing is," I grinned without taking my focus off his flushed face, "the girl makes me hard as fuck —but she's only seventeen and off limits. While I'm fond as fuck of breaking the law when it comes to computers and extortion—" I flatlined my lips "— I'm not a dick. The last thing I want to do is hurt a young woman who's been hurt enough already."

A muscle in Ryker's jaw twitched his beard.

"She might not want or need a fuck buddy right now, but I *am* going to be her friend if she'll let me, Ryker," I told him, dead fucking serious. "And if months down the road *she* decides she wants to be more, I'm sure as fuck going to give her whatever her little heart desires. She seems the type worth waiting for, and I'm not going to let you or any other Vipers stand in my way of getting my name tattooed over her heart if I can talk her sweet ass into letting me in."

Our stare down lasted for a few more seconds before I clinked my bottle against his and sauntered off, having said my piece, stating my intentions, all but letting the boys know I wanted her—and planned to keep her, given the chance.

Ricky chuckled something about me being pussy whipped as I sauntered off, and even though I hadn't gotten a taste of her, I had to agree.

Dasia caught sight of me, her face flushing when she noticed I headed straight toward her.

I half expected an arm to grab mine and spin me around—Ryker demanding I keep my distance, but he didn't.

There was no question I unnerved the girl. She licked her lower lip, glancing toward Pia beside her, before turning toward me once more, shaking hands clasped in front of her. She offered a smile which also trembled, and I wondered over the internal struggle her eyes revealed taking place inside her head.

I expected she felt like damaged goods, full of fear and maybe even self-hatred, thinking her choices may have been what caused the shit that slammed into her life the previous couple of months.

Fuck knew I dealt with the same shit whenever memories managed to escape that prison I locked them up inside me.

I tried like fuck to keep the lust from my eyes while returning her smile and stopping a few feet away from her personal space that I expect she'd want.

"Hey," she squeaked.

"How are you doing?" My voice came out a bit uneven, and I realized she affected me almost as much as I did her.

Her gorgeous tits rose high as she filled her lungs. "You making small talk or really want to know?" she asked with a rush before snapping her lips shut, her face turning even redder.

She gulped as my smile widened.

"Ryker said you're taking classes at Stone's dojo and starting work at the shop this coming week."

"Yeah." Dasia rubbed her palms down her jeans as I'd seen her do twice already since she'd dropped off a plate at the dessert table.

"Sounds as though outwardly you're doing pretty well."

"Mmm." She nodded, flitting her focus over to Pia who stood chatting with Shaun a few feet away.

"Ryker told me what happened."

She snapped her attention back to my face. "Yeah?"

I shoved my free hand in my jeans pocket. "Just wanted to tell you that if you ever need anything, I'll be there for you, okay?"

"I sleep with your sweatshirt," she blurted and grasped her cheeks. "Oh, God. I mean, I'll give it back—I just really appreciated the gesture, is all."

My lips twitched, drawing her focus to them. She jerked her attention back up quick as fuck, eyes slightly widened, pupils telling me all I needed to know.

Goddamn.

My dick attempted to swell, but I cleared my throat, determined to keep a tight rein on myself. "You can keep it."

"Th-thanks," she whispered, once more ripping her gaze off me to glance around the huge yard. "You guys do this often?" Her voice shook as she seemed desperate to change the topic.

"Not really, no. Just haven't gotten together since our camping trip up to Maine earlier this summer."

Pia turned enough to see me, and her attention shot toward where I'd left Ryker before returning to me, her smile unsure. "Devil," she said, her voice in agreement with her lips.

"How are you feeling?" I asked, glancing down at her stomach.

"Not sick anymore—and ravenous for a burger." She glanced at Dasia. "Ready to grab some food?"

Dasia nodded and offered me another shaky smile. "See you around."

Her voice hinted at a question, so I nodded.

Better fucking believe it.

5

———

DASIA

I followed along behind Pia and Shaun toward the smoking grills, having to quickly side step two little brats racing past at break-neck speed, their laughter and squeals quickly disappearing as we neared the Bose speakers.

My neck tingled, and I couldn't help myself. I glanced over my shoulder to find Devil still standing where I'd left him, his lips twitching upward.

Caught gawking yet again, but I couldn't help myself. He'd kept his distance while talking to me even though his eyes spoke volumes. The devil himself danced in the darkness of his twinkling eyes, but heat lingered beyond. As a stripper, I'd seen my fair share of lust, but he didn't skeeve me out one bit.

Quite the opposite.

Panties a soaked mess and my pulse still thrumming, I turned away, my eyes still burning with the image of his perfect lips. Full bottom and the curve of the upper had snagged my attention a few times, embarrassing the hell out of me.

The man was hot as hell—and smelled fucking *divine.*

Sweet licorice still teased my nose. I'd wanted to lean in and sniff his neck, along his clean-shaven jaw. Hell, I wanted to bury my face against his skin and feel those veined arms wrap around me.

His sweatshirt would have to do, though.

I chowed down on a hotdog with ketchup—and got teased to hell from Shaun over that fact, but I hated mustard and relish with a passion. The three of us sat at a picnic table with another woman named Giada and two older women whose names I didn't catch.

All old ladies, they called themselves, and the desire to belong as they did twisted my heart.

One of the older ladies asked Pia how she was feeling, and she replied as she'd told Devil about no longer feeling sick which I hadn't paid attention to thanks to his close proximity.

That woman then turned to Shaun, asking the

same question, and my focus dropped toward where Shaun held her hand to her lower belly.

"Never better." Her face glowed as I jerked my attention back upward, my heart stalling out. "Stone painted the guest room this week—pale blue, almost a gray. It matches the bedding. I'm so excited."

I missed the rest of whatever she said as I realized the truth of my situation. Ryker and Pia would be parents. They weren't going to want an outsider bunking out in their guest room. I imagined them bringing home their baby to start a new life—and my being in the way.

Hurt and longing swept in like a Nor'easter, thickening my throat and tightening my chest until I felt the need to wheeze.

Don't cry. Don't cry.

"Bathroom?" I managed to ask Pia while holding in my tears.

"They're just inside the club's back door over there," she said, pointing across the green toward the biggest building inside the compound. "Want me to go with you?"

"No," I rushed to answer, forcing a smile. "Be right back."

I hopped up and made a beeline for the door she'd indicated, ignoring the groups of people I passed, intent on escaping to get hold of myself. Once locked inside the single toilet bathroom, I allowed a good pity cry for all of two minutes before wiping away my tears and using a damp paper towel to fix the mascara mess down my cheeks.

Eighteen was three weeks away, but I could always sneak off with my freedom. Nothing was holding me back—except for the idea that Ivan and his buddies might be looking for me.

What could I do? Without money, I couldn't hop a bus for California. I could always hoof it, but the thought of sticking out my thumb and ending up in another container to be shipped off for a life of submission...

Nope. I would stick around for at least a little while, but I needed to make myself scarce before that baby came.

One big inhale and slow exhale, and I grabbed the door, chin up and ready to face the world.

Devil leaned against the hallway's wall across from the door, arms crossed, his brow furrowed as I pulled up short and his gaze took in my face. "You okay?"

I nodded and stepped into the hallway, letting the bathroom door shut behind me.

"Anything I can do to help?"

My attempted smile wobbled and I shook my head even while considering asking for a hug. God, I needed one. Seriously. At least, I thought I did. I'd never been in a man's arms for comfort before.

Devil straightened, shoving his hands into his pockets in an endearing display of non-aggression or forwardness even though the look in his eyes betrayed his real thoughts.

"I'm going to find the fuckers who did this to you," he said, his tone low, full of determination. "Make sure they'll never hurt another young woman ever again."

Devil didn't even know me, and yet he took my well-being to heart. Because of being Ryker's brother or because he wanted to get inside my pants?

"I hope you do," I said, not sure I fully referred to his statement or the last question still lingering in my head.

His focus slid down to the arms I hadn't realized I'd wrapped around myself, lingering on my chest long enough to pebble my nipples. He licked his lower lip once his gaze reached my eyes once more.

A shiver slid over my bare arms, raising goosebumps.

"Ryker told me to stay away from you."

My eyebrows shot up. "What?"

His slow sexy smirk melted my panties. "He knows I think you're the sexiest woman I've ever seen."

Heat flooded my face. "O-oh. Thank you."

"You've got balls most men would covet, too," he said, and I bit back a light, shaky laugh. "I'm serious. You're one hell of a woman, doing what you did to escape. Can't say I've ever met such a strong person." He shrugged, his eyes twinkling again as he tipped his head to the side. "Gotta admit to admiring you—just a bit."

What should have sounded like a cheesy pick up line didn't give me that impression at all, and God knows I'd heard my fair share at the two strip clubs I'd worked at.

"So, you obviously don't give a fuck about Ryker's orders." I found myself smiling, my self-hug loosening slightly.

"The only way I'm going to stay away from you is if *you* tell me to, Dasia."

Tension simmered to life between us, and I chewed on the inside of my lip. That damn war...

"Not gonna push you," he continued when I didn't answer, "but if you're interested in defying Ryker along with me, you won't hear one complaint from my lips."

Said lips snagged my attention, the soft curve and lingering smirk creating all sorts of fun flutters in my belly.

"I'm not in any frame of mind to even think about getting involved," I said, more for my own mind set than his.

"Then let me be your friend."

"With benefits?" I couldn't help but ask to see where his true intentions lay.

"Only if you want."

Oh, the temptation ... I expected Devil, hot as fuck bad boy biker, could show me what fucking was *supposed* to be like.

"I'd like to be your friend," I whispered what I knew was proper—safe. "But that's it."

He studied my face so intently, I wanted to melt beneath his gaze. "Just for now?"

I couldn't answer, because I didn't know. While a consensual fuck or ten sounded like a kickass time, my soaked panties evidence of that truth, I imagined getting involved with Devil would only leave me with a broken heart.

With those eyes, those lips, he could probably coax any normal woman into his bed. Or bending over his bike. Or dropping to her knees.

God.

A shiver rippled over me, and I focused on the reality of my current life. I wouldn't be staying long term—that much I knew for certain.

Anything beyond friendship wasn't in our cards even if I had the balls he claimed to choose over the aversion my mind felt over my body's desire for him.

"Come on," he said, tipping his head toward the door leading outside. "I caught sight of those brownies you brought. We'll be lucky if all those rug rats left any for the adults."

"They'd better," I said, moving up the hallway, relieved to be thinking and talking about something else. "They're dark fudge—best kind ever."

"No walnuts?"

I grimaced, shaking my head. "Hell, no."

He chuckled and pushed the door outward, the sun warming my face. "Damn right."

Hours passed, and darkness slowly took over the sky. A couple of bon fires lit the area, but it was Devil's continued stare that heated me through. I'd danced on stage, pranced around naked enough to know when a man lusted after me, but with Devil...

That man twisted me up inside in every way imaginable until my head ached. He might think he wanted me, but if he learned the depth of sickness eating away inside my damn brain, he'd take the hell off and never look back.

I'd poured my story out to Pia, but maybe I needed to see a therapist. My body had certainly been on board with whatever Devil had in mind, but my head made my skin crawl even while shivering with excitement.

Twice, during the rest of the night, Devil hung around near Pia, Ryker, and me as groups intermingled and a few of the brothers started laughing and talking louder.

A handful of women ended up dancing like I'd expected, and the itch to join them had my knee hopping while I leaned onto the picnic table, chin propped up in my palm.

Giada and Shaun both joined in the dancing, asking me to come along with them, but I declined, knowing Devil's gaze would be plastered on me. For the first time in my life, self-doubt over my dancing burrowed into my brain.

I didn't need any man's attention on me. Didn't want it in *that* way.

But, maybe that would someday change. Maybe *I* would change, and my body and head would be on the same page, willing to trust a man enough to let him in.

Hope clung like a stubborn bitch, especially as Ryker lay his hand on Pia's lower back as they went upstairs to bed a few hours later, leaving me alone in their living room. He'd had an aversion to touch when they'd first met, Pia had confided in me. And even though he still had issues here and there, she told me he was a different man. Healed for the most part and thriving in their newfound love.

Perhaps I would heal one day, too. Perhaps one day the broken part of me would be glued back together and I could find my knight in shining armor.

Curling up in bed a short time later, Devil's sweatshirt against my nose, I prayed it was possible.

6

DEVIL

I heard through the grapevine—Sully while at the cook out—that Dasia was going to work in the chop shop's office starting Monday. Even though I knew Ryker would be around, I knew he enjoyed greasing up his hands with his head under a hood. He wouldn't hover over Dasia in the office all day, and I needed to be around her somehow.

Besides, my showing up at the compound wouldn't be out of the ordinary. Fuck knew I spent enough time there since I had nobody and nothing but computers to keep me company at home.

The chop shop sat at the back of the compound's acreage which bordered state land to keep prying eyes from taking too much interest in our going ons. I parked at the edge of the gravel lot alongside the shop—closest to the office door. Bag and drink carrier in hand, I hunched up a bit in my sweatshirt against the colder breeze, and hurried to the locked door.

Praying Ryker wouldn't answer and I'd have at least a few seconds to talk to Dasia, I pressed the intercom button with my elbow.

"Yes?" a female voice I recognized answered, bringing an all-out grin to my face.

"It's Devil, and I come bearing gifts."

"What kind of gifts?"

I chuckled. "Coffee and dark fudge brownies."

A buzz and click sounded, and I shoved the bag beneath my arm to wrench open the door.

Dasia sat across the office behind Ryker's desk, the sight of her smile, pink cheeks, and bright blue eyes fresh without a hint of makeup slamming me in the chest.

Holy fuck, she did strange things to me.

"Hey," she said as I moved into the office, completely fucking enchanted by the little redhead whose memory I'd jerked off to the night before —twice.

"Hey, back." I set the bag and coffees onto the desk without taking my eyes off hers. "You're beautiful."

She laughed lightly, seemingly much more at ease than Saturday at the cookout. "Thanks."

She even knew how to take a damn compliment.

"You look like a cream and extra sugar kinda girl," I said, handing her one of the coffees.

Her smile widened, and she reached for the cup, her fingers grazing against mine.

My dick twitched even though I'd emptied my goddamn balls less than an hour earlier—to thoughts of Dasia tied to my bed, thighs spread wide, and panting. Begging.

I cleared my throat and ripped my attention off her plump lips as she sipped. "Ryker around?" I asked, glancing toward the door leading into the shop. Glass made up the top portion, but I didn't see his ugly mug beyond.

"Yeah. He's actually tuning up an old Kia of Sully's. Said I could have it for a couple hundred bucks."

"You'll have your own wheels."

"For the first time, ever." Happiness coated every word leaving her lips, and I turned to find her eyes revealing a depth of vulnerability I'd yet to see on her face.

While I didn't want to kill the mood, I wanted to know Dasia fucking inside and out. Needed to burrow deep if I wanted to infiltrate her life in the way I planned on doing—legally and consensually. *Eventually.*

My balls and dick ached for those three weeks to pass, but I would give her however fuck the long she needed to let her walls down and allow a man touch her again.

"Ryker tells me you've been in foster care your whole life."

"Until recently, yeah."

"It's a fucking shame—your mom has no fucking clue what she gave up."

Lips pursed, all hint of her smile gone, Dasia glanced at the bag I still held in my hand. "That for me?"

I handed it over, letting her take the lead if she didn't want to talk. "No walnuts."

She pulled the brownie out, sank her teeth into it, and the resulting moan set me at full mast, ready to fucking go.

"So, how's work?" Even I heard the strain in my voice while I fought the urge to adjust my bulge.

"Good." She glanced around the dusty office with its knickknacks, old filing cabinets dented from fists and who knew what the fuck else, and the paper riddled desk in front of her. "This isn't a legit shop, is it?" she asked and took another bite as I pretended to straighten one of the club pictures across the office from her.

I shrugged and lounged onto the chair beneath the picture. "You'll have to ask your boss that one. He at least paying you good money?"

"Good enough to keep my lips sealed shut, yeah," she said around her mouthful. "Under the table, too."

Said boss man pushed into the office, glaring when he noticed my sitting there. "The fuck you doing here?"

"Relax, Ryker. I'm just hanging out with my new friend," I told him with a grin while motioning toward Dasia. "Brought her a brownie since we missed out on hers Saturday."

He grunted something about only being seventeen.

"I brought a black, bitter coffee for your grumpy ass, too."

"Thanks," he muttered, picking the other cup off the desk. "You okay, kid?" he asked Dasia.

She smiled while glancing at me and nodded. "Yeah."

"This cocksucker bothers you, let me know. I'll break his pretty face for you."

She blinked up at Ryker, her eyes widening. "Don't you dare!"

Ryker's scowl deepened. "Fuck." He glanced over at me and pointed toward the door. "Break time's over. She's got work to do."

I stood and sauntered toward the door, but took an eyeful of Dasia before pulling it open. "See ya later, Jail Bait."

The music of her laughter followed me through the door, cutting off too damn abruptly as it slammed shut behind me as though Ryker kicked it. Chuckling, I tucked my chin into my sweatshirt and hurried back toward my truck.

———

I dialed up Stone as soon as I pulled my F250 into my garage twenty minutes later. "Got an opening in that morning karate class?" I asked him.

"What?"

"I feel like I'm getting fat." I pinched at next to nothing but skin on my abs.

He huffed a snort. "Your skinny ass is fucking ripped."

"Wouldn't mind knowing how to fight like you," I tried again. "I'm good with a damn keyboard, but not my fists. I need you to turn me into a badass mother-fucker, brother."

"Planning on getting into a fight sometime soon?"

I considered Ryker's protectiveness over Dasia and wondered if it would last after she turned eighteen. Knowing him, it would. "I wouldn't be surprised if a bloody nose or three lay in my future."

He laughed. "Just stay the fuck away from her, you stupid fuck."

"Don't know what you're talking about," I said, shoving my truck door open.

"You couldn't keep your damn eyes off her Saturday."

"She's hot as fuck, what can I say?"

"She's also just as hot for you—but if you don't want to fuck up that already hawk-like nose any more, I'd do as Ryker says and keep your damn paws off."

"We're just friends."

"Uh huh, and Giada's ugly as shit."

I let myself into my house, making tsking noises. "I'm telling her you said that."

"Fuck off, Devil."

"Sign me up for Dasia's class, and my lips are sealed."

"Stay the fuck away from Dasia or I'll tell Ryker."

"Goddamnit, Stone. Help a brother out!"

"I am—Ryker. Dasia's too young for your ass."

I scowled while kicking my door shut. "I'm only thirty for fuck's sake."

"Twelve years difference."

I tossed my keys onto the island. "And Warden has sixteen on Shaun so what's your real issue here?"

"If I need to say it out loud, then I'm right."

"Fuck off," I grumbled and hung up before he could spout off any new shit I didn't already know.

Dasia was damaged goods and I had a kink that would probably set her off. But maybe I was exactly what she needed. Still grumbling, I stomped up the stairs for the office—and my monitors that didn't judge or bark orders at me.

A few clicks and I sat back grinning—that tiny camera on top of the picture across from Dasia's new desk wasn't in color, but good enough to feed my obsession.

Jail bait if I got found out—but I knew how to cover my ass.

Sick fuck, too—but I enjoyed the hell out of watching her clean off Ryker's desk anyway.

7

DASIA

I had wheels, and even though both Ryker and Pia didn't like my going anywhere alone, by the end of the week they let me go to my karate class without an escort. Ryker had claimed everything was quiet on the Ivan front as far as he and his brothers knew—I also found out that Devil was their tech nerd, but he was as far from nerd looking as one could be in my opinion.

His sweatshirt still wrapped around me at night, but hardly a remnant of his scent lingered. I still found comfort in it, though, remembering how he'd been so careful and cautious when offering it to me.

A good man, I told myself even while another part of me claimed he was a naughty boy.

Either way, he turned me on, and whenever I

couldn't sleep, I found myself thinking of him and those bedroom eyes and curved lips while touching myself. Twice I dreamed he'd been the one to tie me up, and I woke with my heart pounding but not from fear. Both times, my panties were a sopping mess, too.

Sick.

Frowning, I parked in front of the dojo and grabbed my water bottle off the passenger seat. Pia had suggested I speak with a therapist, but Ryker shot that shit down since he didn't want anyone knowing where I was. He even had Stone and Sensei Jason calling me by a different name—DeeDee for Dasia Diane. I'd have preferred a whole different name, but whatever. The man let me stay at his house for free and fed me, too.

Listening to them go at it sometimes, though...

Headboard banging wasn't so bad, but Ryker did not know how to keep quiet. In all the foster homes I'd been in, I'd never heard a man make so much damn noise when fucking.

Kinda skeeved me the hell out, but Pia's voice always rose in the end too, and as long as she was happy, I decided to not give a fuck. A pillow over the head sufficed somewhat. Better than nothing, anyway.

Blowing out a heavy exhale to rid my mind of thoughts of them fucking and ready for karate, I hopped out of my new old car, waving at one of the moms who headed toward the building—Lini, I think her name was.

"DeeDee!"

I turned to find another classmate loping toward me, a goofy grin on his face. "Hey, Jack."

A not pleasant shiver slid over me as he did a quick up and down over my body with his shit brown eyes, but I kept my smile in place, not wanting to make any waves that would bring attention to me.

"Looking good, girl," he said, elbowing me as I continued toward the dojo's front door.

"Thanks," I forced myself to mutter.

He didn't hop forward to get the door for me, so I pulled it open, his whistle and something groaned about my ass directly after turned my stomach.

I hurried toward the far end of the dojo and Sensei Jason who chatted with another class mate. I also waited until Jack took a place on the mats so I could pick one on the opposite side.

We had to partner up for part of the class, and I latched onto Lini like a lifeline, especially since Jack blatantly checked me out non-fucking stop throughout class. I'd taken note of him the first two classes, but had been too caught up in my own nervousness over the newness of karate to pay much attention to a leering guy.

But that Friday? Yeah. Skeeve city.

I hung close to Lini, even exiting the building with her after Jack had left. Lini took off before I realized the leering asshole had pulled his car up alongside mine.

He cranked down his window when I neared, but I ignored him, focusing on the keys in my hand and the lock my shaking hand would need to shove it into.

"DeeDee!" he called.

"What?" I hollered back without looking at him.

"Grab some breakfast with me."

"Can't. Gotta work."

"Come on, girl."

I heard his car door shut, and fuck unlocking and trying to get myself in my car—I turned and hurried back toward the dojo, my heart racing so damn bad my throat wanted to close off.

"DeeDee!"

"Forgot something!" I half-squeaked while hurrying away from him, thoughts of Ivan getting me in his car only to knock me out with a fist giving me an adrenaline rush I didn't know how to handle.

I shook from head to toe, and a sob caught in my throat as Sensei Jason's gaze landed on me. He frowned and met me halfway across the dojo even though the next class lingered around, eyeing me like I was a damn psycho or something.

"What's wrong?" he asked, grasping both my arms gently and leaning down to look into my eyes.

"J-just got spooked..."

He knew enough from Stone to figure out what I'd meant, and grasped my hand. "Come on."

Once inside his office, he handed me a box of tissues so I could wipe up the tears on my face.

"Want me to call Ryker?" he asked, arms crossed and looming over me as I slumped in a chair, the adrenaline crash leaving me a shaking mess.

"Devil," I whispered on a rushed exhale.

Sensei Jason picked up his phone without question while I considered my request. Ryker would protect me to the death, I had no doubt, but he left me feeling a little nervous. Not in a bad way, just afraid he'd kill whatever guy made me uncomfortable. I couldn't have that with Pia being pregnant.

Devil seemed just as adamant about having my back, so...

"Was it Jack?" Sensei Jason asked. "I've seen him watching you."

"Yeah. I don't think he really meant me any harm, but still."

"You okay to hang in here until Devil shows up?"

I nodded up at him. "Yeah. Thanks—and sorry about that."

"Don't worry about it." He patted my shoulder. "I'll check outside to see if Jack's still here and give him an earful, alright?"

Again, I nodded but also managed a whispered, "Thanks again," before he left me alone.

Slumping down farther into the seat, I let out a heavy exhale and closed my eyes, tipping my head against the back of the chair.

How long would I carry around the bullshit? How long did PTSD last? I needed to talk to a damn therapist—Ryker would just have to get over it. Weren't there patient privilege rights or some such shit to help protect me? No one would even know I went to a damn therapist unless I spilled the damn beans myself.

Ryker let me go to karate, so what was the damn difference?

By the time Devil showed up, I'd calmed to almost normal except the butterflies of knowing I would see him. He came barreling into the office and dropped to his knees in front of me before I lost my breath at the sight of him.

His brow furrowed deeply, rage in his eyes as he peered up at me. "You okay?"

"Yeah." I tried for a smile to ease him a bit, but it wobbled at best.

"The fucker was already gone when Jason got outside—Jack's his name?"

I nodded.

"I'm gonna kill the fucker."

A huff of laughter came out along with another onset of tears. "He didn't do anything—just freaked me out for a minute is all." I swiped at the tears rolling down my cheeks, and Devil stood, pulling me right up and out of the chair.

Those arms—that scent—dear lord. Even if I *had* a vibranium shield to protect me from Devil, it would fail. Terribly so.

I clung to his sweatshirt, my tears soaking his front as he held me with tenderness, his hot breath against the top of my head, the sweetness of licorice filling my nose with every snuffled inhale.

Even though the tears continued, my body took note of his warmth, his muscles, the damn hardness of his pec beneath my cheek. Panties well on their way to being a sopping mess, I continued to hold on tight. Soaking in the type of hug I'd never had from a man before.

Kind of addicting...

I finally stopped with the tears, taking stock of Devil plastered to my front—from head to toe—and all the good bits in between.

He was hard against my belly, but didn't grind. Didn't hump like a dog like some of the boys I'd dated—and even Mr. Griffey when he'd gotten too close.

So why didn't Devil's attention and erection freak me out? What about him turned me on, creating a deep ache inside me?

I sighed, wishing I could soak right through his skin and hide out inside him until the whole Ivan and Russian thing settled down so I could live a normal life again.

"Sorry I stink," I mumbled against his sweatshirt, eyes still closed.

"I think you smell fucking fantastic."

That actually got a light laugh out of me, and he pulled back enough to smooth my hair away from my face and study my eyes. "Better now?" he asked, his voice rough, rasped, and rumbling. Panty melting.

Light brown eyes—more amber than Jack's shit color—enticed my head to la-la land, and I stared. Lost.

Zero skeeving, just pure lust.

My pulse sped back up to adrenaline pumping speed as his focus dropped to my lips. Did mine part? Did I dart out my tongue to wet the lower?

Maybe. Probably.

He groaned and pulled back enough that our bodies no longer touched, leaving my front cold. "Goddamnit, Jail Bait, you're gonna be the death of me."

"Sorry," I whispered, glancing away rather than down to check out his bulge like I really wanted to. My arms found their way around my midsection as he exhaled an unsteady breath and ran a hand through his hair.

"Need a fucking haircut," he grumbled when he caught me looking at his mussed hair.

"Don't."

One of his eyebrows cocked upward.

"Looks good long on top like that," I explained with a shrug while heat flooded my face. Could I be any more obvious? Between barking at Ryker not to mess up Devil's pretty face and my telling him I liked his hair ... might as well add tight nipples in, too. At least my gi covered the girls.

"Want to go grab some coffee and brownies?"

My heart did a little flop at the boyish charm his smile flashed at me. "I gotta get to work. I'm surprised Pia hasn't called yet. This is the first time they've let me drive here alone."

As if I summoned her, the throw away cell Ryker had bought for me chimed in my bag. I dug it out to find a text.

Pia: **Where are you?**

Me: **Still at dojo—will be back soon.**

"Got a cell, huh?" Devil asked as I tucked my phone back into my bag and grabbed it off the floor alongside the chair I'd occupied.

"Yeah. Ryker gave it to me."

"Going to give me your number?" That flashing smile did me in, again.

Ryker wouldn't be happy, I had a feeling, but I found myself nodding.

Five minutes later, I pulled out of the dojo's parking lot, Devil on my tail in his big blue truck—just in case. Guess he didn't like me heading off on my own either. He told me he would stop by the shop later to put a tracking device on both my cell and car.

Feeling protected and resting in that fact, I drove to my temporary home and waved when Devil left once I'd reached the stoop.

I was confused beyond help, but kept that to myself when telling Pia what had happened.

When I got to the shop forty-five minutes later, I learned Pia had filled Ryker in. He called Stone and told him to put the fear of God in that Jack fucker, or he would. He also gave me shit for asking for Devil rather than him, and I broke down and told him the real reason.

Pia was like a mom to me, I explained, and I couldn't have her raising that child alone.

That quieted him up quick as hell, and tight-lipped, he left me alone in the office.

Devil showed up as promised, subs and tonic in hand. He'd bought for the crew, though, so Ryker, Sully, and two prospects without nicknames crammed into the office with us since it had started to rain.

The men joked and bullshitted with one another while we ate, holding nothing back with a young woman in the room, making me feel as though I truly belonged there.

I might be sick, but I began to think that perhaps the shit of my life the previous few months might have been worth it. I'd found a family of sorts, the kind I'd always longed for.

Glancing over at Devil while thinking this, I found him staring at me and sipping his tonic. He flashed a smile around his straw, tightening everything inside me in the best way possible.

Okay, so maybe I longed for just a bit more.

8

DEVIL

A couple more days passed without me able to find any connection to the Russian mafia, the sex slave operation we assumed they ran, and Martínez. All remained quiet on the Vegas front as well, Ryker reported, but an underlying unease we all agreed upon lingered.

I needed to find the connections without stirring up dust that would leave footprints back to the Vipers, and I'd never met such a challenge. When needing breaks, I checked in on the shop's camera, watching Dasia work for a few minutes. I'd hooked up her phone and car with tracking devices, and she told me she felt much safer.

Ryker began allowing her to drive to karate alone again, but he didn't know I trailed at a distance anyhow. Jack didn't so much as look in her direction whenever they showed up at the dojo at the same time. I wasn't sure who told him to stay the fuck away from Dasia, but they had my appreciation.

I finally talked Stone into letting me join, and that Monday I showed up for class—unannounced to Dasia—her face flushed the prettiest pink, I had a hard time talking my dick down.

She became my partner whenever Sensei Jason required us to find one. Gave me the opportunity to touch her here and there, nothing inappropriate lest I scare the girl.

That day in the office when she'd cried in my arms, she'd known how she affected me. There was no hiding my aching dick, but she hadn't pulled away. At least she didn't have touch issues like Ryker. Fuck knew how Pia helped get him out of that funk.

I didn't push even though I wanted to. Sure, I crowded up in her wheels sometimes, making her shiver and pupils blow out wide, but I kept my hands and dick to myself.

One week before her eighteenth birthday, Ryker left the shop for a doctor's appointment with Pia, leaving her alone in the office while Sully and the other two guys worked.

I texted her the second he left the compound.

Me: **What are you up to, Jail Bait?**

Sitting back in my chair, feet propped up on my desk, ankles crossed, I watched her snatch up her cell from her bag. She smiled, her fingers flying over the screen.

Jail Bait: **Working. You?**

Me: **Thinking about you.**

I sent the text and brushed my knuckles down the back of my semi beneath my jeans. While I was a sick fuck for watching her throughout the day without her knowing, at least I hadn't taken to jacking off right there at my desk while doing it. Even I wasn't that much of a perv.

Dasia nibbled on her lip but didn't make a move to reply, so I continued with my own trail of thoughts.

Me: **And what color panties you're wearing. Or not wearing.**

She bent over her phone.

Dasia: **You would.**

Me: **Got that fucking right. I also think about sliding them down off your legs.**

Couldn't fucking help it—I loved to get her riled up, get that pulse thrumming in her neck when I got too close.

Dasia tipped her head back and appeared to laugh while mouthing, "Oh, my God."

She didn't look pissed, so I decided to test my luck.

Me: **Touching you. Tasting you.**

That got another lip nibble out of her while she stared at the phone.

Dasia: **You're really fresh.**

Me: **Tell me you wouldn't love it. Tell me you don't touch yourself thinking about that very thing.**

I'd never pushed her that far, but I had to know. Fuck, I had to know.

She shifted on the chair before answering.

Jail Bait: **You'd like for me to admit that wouldn't you?**

Me: **Damn right.**

Jail Bait: **Well I don't. "Just friends" don't do that shit.**

In the mood to argue, I let my fingers fly.

Me: **Don't have to stay platonic if you don't want to. Just sayin'.**

Jail Bait: **I'm only 17.**

Me: **Not for long.**

A week, actually. In just over a week Dasia would be a consenting adult in the eyes of the law—not that I truly gave a shit. Given the green light, I'd have been all over her plump ass and those tits.

She put her phone down, and I groaned, hating I couldn't get what I wanted out of her. At least give a blue-balled guy something to hang his coat on other than his raging hard-on.

Dasia went into the tiny bathroom while I squeezed my dick to calm the fuck down. She took long enough I started to wonder if she was okay, but she came back out and didn't even look at her damn phone.

Grumbling, I turned off my obsession and all but one monitor of her and picked up where I'd left off looking for that fucker Ivan.

Three long as fuck hours later, I found him. But his real name was Alexi Dvornikov—and he happened to be a good buddy of the asshole the Vipers had buried out in Vegas alongside Arturo.

A pain in the ass slip through the FBI's database backdoor earned me that information, but at least there was no mention of the demise of the fucker Stone had taken out with his knives.

Alexi, the FBI hadn't yet confirmed, ran the Russian mob's sex slave trade. I fucking ran with what they had, searching other databases I snuck into when necessary. Emails. Phone records. Bank records and home security.

Things began to pop up, and I saved every tiny shred of evidence I thought might help build the FBI's case to finally free Dasia from having to live in fear. Until I finished for the night, I'd missed dinner and crawled into bed hours after most.

At least my obsession to protect Dasia had proven a good thing. I had the beginnings of the necessary shit to take all the fuckers down.

9

DASIA

"So, what do you want to do for your birthday next weekend?"

I lifted my head from the plate of lasagna in front of me to meet Pia's smile. "I honestly hadn't thought about it." Well, I had thought about the whole being legal thing and what that could possibly bring about between me and Devil, but I hadn't considered the actual day.

"Want me to make you a cake?"

"Brownies would be nice," I said with a grin.

"You and your brownies," Ryker said, shaking his head without a lick of humor on his face. God knew he hated whenever Devil showed up at the office with a bag of them for me.

"You ought to try one," I told him. "Chocolate can do wonders for one's disposition."

Pia snorted, and I chuckled as Ryker raised an eyebrow my way.

"Hey." I shrugged. "Works for PMS, figured it wouldn't hurt to maybe shove one in your face."

His lips twitched, but he returned to his lasagna, forking up a bite.

Still laughing, I turned back toward Pia. "Brownies and black coffee for the man of the house."

While Ryker still unsettled me with his intensity in protecting what belonged to him, I'd come to like his poppa bear attitude. He was badass, don't get me wrong, but I'd learned he had a soft inside. Squishy and heart-eyed when it came to his old lady.

He'd even allowed me to contact my best friend Stacey with the promise I wouldn't tell her where I was. We talked for over two hours the night before, and even though I couldn't give names or even hint that I was with a motorcycle club, I told her about the man I'd met, the one who drove me insane, the one who made me want to submit at his feet when that was the last thing I should want.

Ever.

She claimed I wasn't sick—just horny with a

kinky side. She had one of her own, but my nose wrinkled when she talked about getting spanked by her long-time boyfriend.

Pain play? No thank you.

"I wanted to get you something nice," Pia said, bringing me back to their kitchen, "but wasn't sure what. Once things settle down, I expect you'll want to head out to see the world. Enjoy your freedom finally."

Sadness hinted behind her smile, and even though the thought of leaving their house hurt my heart, too, I knew I couldn't stay.

"Haven't really thought about that, either."

She nodded and went back to dinner while Ryker picked up the kitchen's TV remote to turn it up.

He had a thing with watching the weather—determined to ride his Harley wherever he went, whenever possible. Bundled up like a bear, he headed out every morning on his loud bike at the same time I left for karate.

Clear skies, a bit warmer, the weather girl's voice came from behind me.

The newscaster took over, her voice way too chipper for the headlines she dropped. Another teenage girl disappeared from the Boston area—that made six in the previous three months.

At the mention of Griffey Industries, my heart stuttered, and I glanced up, the half-chewed bite of lasagna in my mouth losing its flavor.

I'd heard he'd jetted for overseas or some such shit, leaving his wife for a younger woman, and hadn't been surprised.

Ryker stared at the TV above me, his usual scowl in place.

Ted Griffey still hadn't been found, the woman behind me continued, and an investigation had begun into his disappearance.

I glanced over to find Pia watching Ryker.

"They never found him overseas with his mistress?" I asked, drawing Pia's attention to my face.

She blinked once. Twice. And turned toward Ryker as though hoping he would answer.

He flicked off the TV and went back to eating without a peep—not even the usual curses whenever my past came up in his presence.

I turned toward Pia once more, and she gave me that hidden smile again, lifting one shoulder in a half-shrug. "I guess not."

Uh huh.

I glanced between the two a few more times as

they ate, my mind having a heyday with the weird vibe I got off both of them.

I'd told Pia Mr. Griffey had touched me inappropriately, and a day later, he's in the hospital after being mugged. The night he got home, he apologized to me. I'd also learned much later than not long after the rape, he'd gone overseas.

Supposedly.

Ryker hunched over his plate, and a nagging thought rippled through my head. He and his brothers were wicked protective of their own, and if he'd already claimed Pia in his head by that point in time, whatever she cared about became his problem. I'd been around him long enough to know that to be fact.

I hated to admit it, but that kinda turned me on.

My cell dinged, and I pulled it out of my pocket.

HAF: **Can't stop thinking about you.**

My face heated as I imagined him stroking himself like he claimed to do when thinking about me. He'd told me that very thing in karate class earlier that morning.

"Stacey?" Pia asked, and I shook my head.

"No." I couldn't very well say *Hot as Fuck* as I'd nicknamed Devil. God knew how Ryker would react. "It's Devil," I decided to go with the truth.

I glanced up to find Ryker's scowl deepened. Big surprise.

"We're just friends," I rushed to assure him.

"I don't trust that fucker," he grumbled, snatching another piece of garlic bread from the basket between us.

"He hasn't done anything inappropriate," I said, lifting my chin, hoping to portray more confidence than I felt since he sure as hell *said* inappropriate things on occasion—especially when sparring in karate.

"He bothers you, you let me know."

I nodded even though I knew I would do no such thing. Ryker had softened my thoughts toward him in the short time I'd lived under his roof, but even if Devil *had* bothered me, I wouldn't have told him.

He peered across the table at me, his eyes cold enough to send a shiver down my spine. I wondered if those were the last things Mr. Griffey saw before drawing his last breath.

I kinda hoped it was.

"I gotta head down to the club later. Want to go along?" Ryker asked, and I sat a little straighter, glancing at Pia like a kid whose parents had asked if the other wanted to go for ice cream.

"If you want us to, sure," she replied for both of us.

He grunted an affirmative.

Biting back my grin, my fingers flew over my cell's screen.

Me: **Heading to the Viper's club after dinner. C U there?**

HaF: **Already here—and now I'm hard again.**

Laughter escaped me, and I swore Ryker grumbled something about killing that fucker.

10

DEVIL

I'd texted the officers earlier in the day, telling them I finally got a fucking lead. Vigil called a meeting, and I headed over to the club early in need of chilling the fuck out.

Two beers in, and I still couldn't stop thinking about Dasia and how much longer it would be before Ryker showed with her and Pia in tow.

Warmer weather had moved in with a fucking awesome jet stream, so once more we lingered around outside by a bonfire, but with a ton less people than the party two weeks earlier.

My dick sprang to attention the second I laid eyes on Dasia in her skinny jeans hugging an ass so damn fine I went light-headed as shit. I couldn't wait to get my hands on that ass... Lick and bite every damn inch while she lay trussed up and shivering, skin pebbled, nipples straining.

Our eyes met as she neared the fire enough I could see her face, and I bit back a groan while adjusting my swollen dick.

She'd gone without makeup, leaving her fresh faced just like I claimed to love every morning before karate.

Ryker eyed me, but I ignored him and headed toward where Vigil and Ricky sat a ways away in the dark. The last to arrive, Ryker followed—but didn't say a word to me.

"Whatcha got?" Vigil asked once the officers all stood together in a tight circle.

I laid out what I'd found so far—the evidence to link the mob, Martínez, and the fucker who'd kidnapped Dasia.

"Is it enough to get their asses hauled in and put away?" Vigil asked.

"Not enough I'd bet money on it, no."

"Fuck," Ryker muttered, knowing I didn't bet money lightly.

"But I've connected the dots the damn FBI hadn't even numbered yet. It's only a matter of time until I have what we need."

"Some fucking footage—goddamn pictures of that fuck tossing women into containers would be nice," Ryker said.

"And if we knew where Dasia had been held, I'd be all over that shit."

"Maybe you ought to take her for a little drive down to the harbor," Stone suggested. "Snoop around and see if it pokes her memory."

While a good idea, his suggestion twisted my guts.

"No." Ryker left no opening for argument in his tone. "Damn girl's been through enough. She's finally starting to relax sitting at a table with me. Even smiling and joking. Won't have that fucked with."

"You mean Pia won't have that fucked with," Ricky tossed out. "You pussy-whipped fucker."

Vigil slapped his hand on Ryker's chest as he took a step forward toward his brother.

Ryker halted, glaring at our president.

"Calm your tits," Vigil said, removing his hand. "Nothing wrong with wanting whatever your old ladies wants—something dipshit over there hasn't learned yet."

"Don't see an old lady on the back of *your* bike," his younger brother snipped back.

"Fuck." Vigil laughed. "You need to get laid."

"Fuck off, Frankie."

The whole circle got real quiet. Ricky never called Vigil by his real name unless ready to toss down and go all out, something they'd done countless times since I'd joined the Vipers.

I stepped into the center of the ring, absolute fucking zero interest in watching fists fly when the little blue-eyed beauty waited for me over by the fire. "I'll have what we need soon," I said, changing the subject and clasping a hand on Ricky's shoulder. "Let's go get a drink."

I dragged him off with me, but Vigil didn't say shit about the treasurer—me—adjourning the meeting.

Keeping my eyes on Dasia, I grabbed both Ricky and I another beer from the cooler we'd brought outside. I handed one off to our VP, and he grumbled a thanks before heading into the club. He'd been living in one of the rooms upstairs for almost two years now, but rarely showed his face unless his brother called a meeting.

I made my way over to Dasia who sat on a blanket a few feet from the fire, her arms wrapped around her upturned knees.

She patted the empty spot beside her when I neared, and I sprawled out on my side, propped up on an elbow while facing her.

"How are ya, Jail Bait?"

Her laughter warmed my fucking heart. "You've really got it bad."

"Damn right." I swigged around my grin. "Anyone ever tell you that you throw a punch like the Black Widow?"

She blinked down at me, and her smile widened. "Are you a Scarlet or Avengers fan?"

"Already told you I was a total nerd."

"Get. Out."

"Thor's my man."

Dasia snorted in laughter. "Fight him for ya."

I held up my hands in defeat. "Share?"

I'd never seen such beautiful, lively eyes, like a summer sky full of promise as she smiled at me. "Share. Hmm. Wouldn't *that* be something."

One of my eyebrows shot up at the lust in her eyes. "Kinky girl."

She turned toward the fire, her smile fading.

"What'd I say?"

"Nothing." She brushed it off, but there was no denying something had hit a nerve.

"So," I said, deciding to let it go, "one more week, huh?"

"Yeah."

"Got any big plans?"

She shrugged, glancing at Pia standing a few feet away with Shaun and Giada. "Not really, no. Pia's making me brownies—my request. Have you found anything?"

"What do you mean?"

"The whole skin trade thing."

I glanced at Ryker who stood with Vigil, his scowl directed at me as usual. "What all has Ryker told you?" I asked, turning to face her once more.

"That you're a genius hacker—"

"He called me a genius?"

"He's called you plenty of not-so-nice names, too."

"Yeah, that sounds about right," I said, lifting my beer to my lips and fighting back a grin.

"He says you're compiling evidence to take down the ring and make it safe for me to live a normal life."

"That's been my focus since you came here, Dasia," I said, pushing up to sit beside her, close enough our elbows brushed.

"Why?" She faced me fully, her eyebrows slightly furrowed. "You don't know me from a hole in the wall. Don't know my past—nothing."

"I'd like to."

11

———

DASIA

My focus dropped to his lips, speeding up my heart rate. I jerked my head back to face the fire as the familiar want and aversion swirled together in my brain.

Tainted. Stained. The usual negatives whispered through my head.

"Do I make you nervous?" he asked, his voice low while leaning just a little closer so our knees brushed.

"A-a little." God, I did *not* know how to talk to real men.

"In a good way or bad way?"

I shrugged, heat creeping up my neck. "You're a tease."

"And given the chance, I'd aim to please."

Oh... My throat didn't want to cooperate when I tried to swallow. "How?" I heard myself whisper, a rush of heat sweeping over me.

Devi let out a low groan and shifted. "Touching you. Tasting you," he quietly repeated what he'd texted me earlier in the week.

My body reacted the same as it had then, but I wasn't about to go to the bathroom as an excuse to secretly get myself off to thoughts of his hands and mouth on my body.

I gulped for air, every inch of my skin on high alert from the heat of his knee and elbow pressing against me. Fully clothed, no skin on skin, and fire hotter than the flames I stared at singed me from the inside out.

"I think about it every hour of the goddamn day," Devil whispered, leaning so close the scent of licorice and hops swarmed over me.

A shiver wracked my body, raising goose bumps along my arms and legs.

"My little Jail Bait—so fucking alluring, I can't get you out of my head. Don't want to."

That damn war inside my head...

"What else do you think about?" I whispered, clinging to the lust side in hopes of winning against the aversion and thoughts of being sick and broken.

"Stripping you down, worshiping every inch of your too-young skin."

My heart skipped a beat, but not at the thought of him doing that very thing. "You want me because you can't have me," I said what his declaration had meant in my head, shifting away and facing him.

Those eyes ... my breath caught at the intensity in his focus, unwavering, full of need.

I inhaled until it hurt, needing to let him know I knew the truth. "If it was two weeks from now you wouldn't—"

"I'd still fucking want you, Dasia."

I stared, completely caught up in the energy crackling between us, the pounding heartbeat in my ears. "How?" I had to ask—had to know.

"In my bed, at my mercy. Sweating. Panting. Tied up tight so I could tease the living fuck out of you and me both."

My eyelids slammed shut, my lips parting to suck in much-needed oxygen as his words kicked off one hell of a fantasy in my mind.

"I want your submission—fucking crave it, Dasia."

Submission. Restraints.

Oh God.

I hopped up, needing space to breathe, to calm

my racing heart as memories of Ivan and his fists slammed into me.

"Dasia?"

Ignoring Devil, I moved toward Pia who chatted with Shaun but watched me.

"Are you alright?" she asked when I got closer, glancing beyond me—probably at Devil.

"Not feeling too great," I managed to wheeze out past the tightness in my chest while fighting the need to wrap my arms around my middle. "Can we leave?"

Pia's brow furrowed, but she slipped an arm around my shoulders. "I'll see you later," she told her friends, and started in the direction of Ryker and the guys he stood with.

"Are you alright?" she whispered again, and I nodded, determined to keep my shit together until we got back to her house.

Ryker noticed Pia first—then me—and his usual scowl dented his brow.

Please don't cause a scene...

"What's wrong?" he barked, and Pia squeezed my shoulder.

"Nothing," she told him. "We're just getting tired."

Ryker glanced behind us, his gaze narrowing. "That fucker upset you?"

"No," I lied, but didn't even bother trying for a smile since my voice probably betrayed me. "Just tired. Long week."

He eyed me long enough I shifted on my feet, glancing away into the dark beyond the compound's fence. My arms found their way around my waist, and I clung tight.

"Go on, Ryker," Vigil said using his head to motion toward the parking lot out front. "Get the ladies out of here. It's late, anyway."

Hardly, I thought, but appreciated his input just the same.

Pia held out her hand, and Ryker laced his fingers through hers before turning and leading the way.

"Thanks," I whispered at the Vipers' president before scampering after them, my backside tingling and my chest still tight as hell.

Fear was a bitch, one I wanted to strangle.

Perhaps it was time to talk to someone other than Pia.

12

DEVIL

I lost control and fucked up. Got too close, breathed in her sweet scent, gave into the first hint of curiosity I'd gotten from her. Fucking caved.

And scared the shit out of her.

Cursing my selfishness, I stared after her as she left the compound on Ryker and Pia's heels. She didn't glance back, merely kept her shoulders hunched as though trying to hide.

Stupid fuck, I cursed myself out while running a hand through my damn hair I still hadn't cut—because Dasia didn't want me to.

At least Ryker hadn't come at me—she must have made an excuse for them to leave as quickly as they did.

Twice, I'd made her uncomfortable, and my

mind quickly recognized the first once the second slapped me in the face. I'd called her a kinky girl then admitted to wanting to tie her up.

While I expected PTSD from the kidnapping fucked with her mind, I should have caught onto that and been more careful with my words.

Heaving a sigh and cursing myself a few more times in my head, I pushed up from the blanket, planning to leave the party behind. Vigil called to me, and I changed my course toward where he still stood with Stone and Warden.

"The fuck did you say to her?" Vigil asked, frowning at me like the fuck up I was.

"Got caught up in our word sparring."

"Mentioned ropes?"

I glanced away. "I might have."

"You stupid fuck."

"Yeah, I've already called myself worse, thanks."

Warden watched me, his brow furrowed while Stone just stared with a blank face.

"Ryker finds out, he's going to kick your ass," Stone said.

Vigil snorted. "He'll do worse than that. You three didn't see what he did to that Griffey fucker—Dasia might not be his flesh and blood, but he's protective as fuck over her."

"You need to make it right," Warden said, his dark eyes staring me down. "We can't have this kind of shit going on right now."

"Why don't you just stay the fuck away from her," Vigil said.

A muscle ticked in my jaw as I peered over to the parking lot and the empty spot where Ryker's truck had sat. "Can't."

My brothers held their silence long enough I turned back toward them. All three stared at me, but I refused to shift under their scrutiny.

"You want her for more than a fuck toy?" Vigil finally asked, and I didn't hesitate to nod. "Then you'd best get your head screwed on straight. Go to Ryker with your intentions. Lay it out—what you want, what you plan."

"And if he says no," Warden interjected, his dark eyes letting me know he'd kick my ass just as fast as Ryker, "then you leave the girl alone."

Leaving Dasia alone wasn't a fucking option. Even if Ryker said no, I wouldn't listen. I had to hear it from *her* lips—had to know what she wanted, not what everyone else wanted for her.

"And if *she* says no, don't push," Stone said. "You're like a goddamn pit bull once you set your mind on something, but she's flesh and blood, not a code to crack or a firewall to find a way through."

I nodded, but knew I would struggle with that last bit of advice as well. Perhaps she and I needed to have a good, old fashioned sit down and work shit out talk.

"I'm heading out," I said, tossing my empty beer bottle into a nearby can.

"Score!" some drunk asshole behind me shouted.

I lifted a hand and took off, my mind made up.

I waited until Ryker's bedroom lights in the front of the house shut off before pulling my truck closer and cutting the engine. I waited another half-hour before climbing out and making my way down the road with nothing but a cool breeze and my soft footfalls to keep me company in the dark.

Ryker lived in a small neighborhood where houses sat a good hundred yards from one another with trees in between to offer privacy. Sneaking up on his ass came easy. Too easy. The fucker didn't even have motion sensor lights around his place.

Deciding on needing to have a little chat with Ryker about his lack of security, I sat in a lounge chair on his back patio and pulled my cell from my sweatshirt's pocket to text Dasia.

Me: **Can we talk?**

I waited, thinking maybe she'd gone to bed and silenced her cell. An owl hooted in the distance as the breeze ruffled my hair. At least it wasn't so cold that my sweatshirt would suffice against the fall night.

My cell buzzed.

Jail Bait: **Sure.**

Me: **In person? I'm out back on the patio.**

Five long as fuck minutes later, the lock on the slider clicked. Dasia shuffled out, quietly sliding the door behind her once more. Her hair tumbled down close to her waist, the brightness of the red dulled by the night. She'd wrapped herself in a thick blanket and wore pink fluffy slippers.

I patted the lounger beside me.

She sat on the edge of the chair facing me, her back ramrod straight. Enough of a moon shone that I could easily make out her face, but not enough to read her eyes to discern her emotional state.

"I'm sorry," I said, keeping my voice low even though I knew Ryker's second floor bedroom lay at the front of the house. "I lost control, and I'm sorry."

"I overreacted."

"No you didn't." My brow furrowed. "Telling you my fantasies was totally inappropriate and insensitive considering what you went through."

She let out a heavy exhale and moved her focus off my face to the woods beyond.

"I was sexually assaulted by our priest when I was a kid," I said what I'd rehearsed in my head on the way over.

Dasia whipped her head back toward me, her brow furrowed deeply. "You were?"

"Yeah." I rubbed my palms on my jeans like she seemed fond of doing, but held her stare. "I was eleven. Mom idolized the fucker and wouldn't listen to my accusations."

"I'm so sorry."

"It's why I crave control now because I had none during that time. Fucking zero." I peered at her, wishing like fuck I could read her face better. "But it's not an excuse for being a prick to you."

"You weren't being a prick." She relaxed a little, her shoulders drooping as she reached to tuck hair behind her ears.

"My Gram believed me and went to the authorities. Either the fucker was loaded or the cops didn't give a shit—the entire thing got swept under the rug. That didn't help my insecurities either."

"I can imagine." She shook her head. "That really fucking sucks."

"While I was a sophomore at MIT, the fucker made the news for abusing another kid. He got off again, and was shown shaking rich fucks hands while walking out of the court house. It was rumored he was good friends with the judge, too. I rebelled, dropped out of college, and that's when I met Vigil."

"He stole your future," she said quietly, pulling her blanket tighter around herself.

"Redirected, yeah, but I love my life. Love the brotherhood I found after dropping out of college. I wouldn't be a Viper if I'd stayed and graduated. I wouldn't be a rich as fuck vigilante who loves making people pay for their sins."

"Making people pay ... as in extortion?"

Club business, but I needed to show her I meant business about *us*. "I'm an outlaw, Dasia. Not as violent as some of my brothers, but I break the law, same as them—on an almost daily basis."

"You're a hacker."

I nodded, pleased to find she didn't frown at that fact.

She straightened. "Can you find the assholes who kidnapped me?"

"Already on it. Gonna make them pay, too."

"Holy shit." She giggled, putting everything inside me back where it belonged. "That's awesome."

"I told you I would protect you—and I meant every word. I'm going to take down the whole ring and everyone connected to it. Mafia and cartel. They're going down for what they did to my girl."

The last part slipped out without intent, but Dasia didn't shy away, her smile fixed firmly in place. "Your girl, huh?"

"Damn right."

"You truly don't give a shit about our age difference do you?"

"Nope."

"The whole restraining thing—it doesn't include that whole pain with pleasure thing, does it?"

"I swear on Gram's life I wouldn't hurt a hair on your head, Dasia. Ever."

She nibbled on her lower lip, and I wanted nothing more than to suckle on the plump flesh and soothe whatever sting she inflicted on herself.

"If you don't think you can handle that kind of relationship," I said when she didn't respond, "tell me now and I'll try like fuck to leave you alone."

"I-I don't want you to leave me alone," she whispered.

"Come here," I said, my voice rasped while holding out my hand.

"I'm only seventeen."

"And I'll wait until next week to bury my dick so far up your young pussy you can't breathe—but I need to touch you, Dasia. Need to hold you in my arms and taste you."

She hesitated, and I cursed my damn runaway mouth. "Shit." I ran my hand through my hair. "Sorry. Didn't mean—"

Dasia scooted off the chair and slid sideways onto my lap before I could blink, her fuckable ass right on my thighs and her face inches from mine.

I groaned and pulled her closer, snuggling her against my swelling dick. She smelled like a spring morning, all fresh and flowery. Burying my face into her hair, I breathed deeply, filling my lungs with her as the silky strands brushed against my nose and cheek.

Wrapping one hand up in the long tresses, I tilted her head back and moved along her neck—fucking smooth as silk skin.

"Tell me to stop and I will," I murmured, flicking my tongue out for the taste I'd been dying for.

"I'm sick," she whispered, and I pulled back to find tears in her eyes.

13

DASIA

"Sick like illness?" he asked, his brow denting the slightest bit.

"No," I rushed to explain, trying to keep the tears from welling too much. "It's just ... I'm broken, Devil."

"Adrian—call me Adrian."

His firm insistence dried my eyes up, and I relaxed against his hard body, soaking in his warmth and the sweet scent of licorice, not caring a blanket, long t-shirt, and panties were the only thing separating my body from his touch. "Okay—Adrian."

"Tell me why you think you're broken."

I tried to study his face in the darkness, but lost the emotion in his eyes to the darkness surrounding us. "I *like* the idea of you tying me up. Restraining me, making me beg—and I shouldn't. I shouldn't want that so damn bad that my body burns, that I ache inside so much I can't breathe."

With a groan, he took my mouth, and I *couldn't* breathe. Soft lips, slick tongue licking along mine... Wetness seeped from my pussy, soaking my panties in a blink as my pulse thundered in my ears.

My blanket dropped to my waist as I grasped his sweatshirt, holding on for dear life.

I'd kissed boys before, but they were exactly that —boys. Adrian destroyed my senses, overrode common sense, carrying my entire body away like a violent ocean with a mere swipe of his tongue. I parted my lips, and he sank in deep with a groan, his hand dropping from my cheek to my thigh, pulling me tighter, every brush of his tongue along mine pulsing energy directly to my clit and tightening my nipples to points.

His hard length dug into my thigh, and I squirmed with need to be closer.

I'd wondered who would ever want a broken soul—and Adrian, the badass biker—answered that for me, clearly and without hesitation. A knight in shining armor, a devil in sheep's clothing.

"We'll be broken together," he murmured against my lips, stinging my eyes again.

Whimpering, I twisted and turned, refusing to let go of his mouth while straddling his thighs. His jeans rubbed the insides of my thighs as I slid in closer until resting my soaked panties against him.

At the brush of his hard cock against my core, I gasped and lifted my head, desperate to see his face, his eyes.

Heavily hooded, they peered at me, attempting to suck my soul from my body.

He grasped my hips and swiveled his own.

"Oh…"

My fingers dug into his shoulders, and I ground against him without thought, panting—needing—uncaring I probably left a wet spot on his jeans.

"How many more days?" he asked, his low tone rumbling and low as he thrust against me like we fucked for real.

"Until?"

"You're eighteen and I won't get my ass tossed in jail for sliding my dick into your sweet pussy."

I gulped, never having known dirty talking was so fucking hot. "S-seven," I gasped as he grabbed my hands and shoved them behind my back, forcing my chest to poke out toward him.

He studied my face as my heart beat in my ears and my lungs sucked in oxygen.

"Okay?"

I licked the sudden dryness from my lower lip and nodded. "Very."

His focus slipped downward to my nipples strained against the thin cotton of my sleep shirt.

Yes, oh, please, yes...

He leaned in and closed his mouth over one.

Fire raced over my skin, and I bit my lip to keep from crying out. My clit throbbed in time with his flicking tongue, and his gentle bite caught my breath.

My hands jerked in his hold, not wanting to escape, but to grasp his head to hold him close. I whimpered and squirmed until he maneuvered both of my wrists into one hand and shoved the other between us.

He palmed my pussy and let out an animalistic growl. "Goddamn, Dasia." His mouth found mine, our lips and tongues frantic, my climax already tingling my toes.

"So wet," he said against my mouth, his fingers dragging along the edges of my panties.

"Please," I moaned, moving against him, desperate for his touch.

He rested his forehead against mine, his fingers continuing to tease. "Please what, Jail Bait?"

"Touch me—my skin."

"But I am."

Another whimper escaped me.

"You mean like this?" He slipped his thumb beneath, and we both groaned as he slid up through my swollen lips to my clit. "So fucking wet." One gentle circle around my throbbing nub, not nearly enough to pitch me over, and he slid back down to circle my dripping core.

I attempted to ride his hand, ached for him to be inside me, but couldn't find words to beg for what I wanted. He teased and teased until tears slid down my cheeks, and he licked them off.

"Do you want to come?"

"Y-yes."

He released my wrists and scooted down on the lounger so damn fast I squeaked, grabbing the chair's arms to keep from toppling over. He grasped my hips and lifted me—right onto his face.

Oh God...

His mouth covered my pussy—through my panties, and my head tipped back as I arched, lower lip between my teeth to keep from moaning too loudly. Nobody had ever gone down on me before, and at the first brush of his tongue along the edge of my panties, twisting to get beneath, my breath left in a rush.

Soft ... so soft.

I spread my thighs as wide as they would go, my arms shaking from my hands' grip to keep me upright.

I shouldn't have worn panties—should have ripped them off before climbing onto his lap—

Adrian shoved them to the side and dove in like a man dying of thirst, his groans and the wet sounds of his sucking on my flesh taking me past the point of no return.

"Adrian..."

"Take what you want, baby." He latched onto my clit, and I bucked against his face, biting down hard on my lip as my climax burst through me like a flash of lightning, currents of energy reverberating over my skin. My pussy pulsed with an ache so damn sweet more tears slid down my cheeks.

The second I sagged atop him, Adrian shifted and moved my limp body back into his arms, holding my cheek to his chest.

His heart pounded against my ear, his cock

digging into my hip. A shiver slid over me along with a sigh as he kissed my forehead.

"Okay?" he whispered.

"Never been better," I heard myself say through the ringing in my ears. "No one has done that to me before."

His groan rumbled against my cheek, tingling through my pussy. "Tell me I can have all your other firsts, Dasia. Fucking tell me."

"Someone already stole that."

"And I'll erase his mother fucking memory—promise."

"I want you to be my first everything else, too, Adrian." I melted against him, my eyes closing in absolute euphoric rightness.

"I want it all, Dasia. Every fucking inch, every tear, every hint of laughter off your lips." He captured my hair again and lifted me off his chest, his dark eyes close enough I could see the black of his pupils ate at the amber brown surrounding them. "You want the goddamn picket fence, it's yours. Walk-in closet? I'll clean my shit out and give it to you. You want a dozen kids? I'll give them to you—or die trying."

"God, no." I couldn't keep from grimacing, the thought of kids almost killing the mood. "No kids."

"Thank fuck." He took my mouth again, and until I crawled into my bed an hour later, my lips bruised and nipples sore, I wished to sleep the week away so my devil could take what belonged to him.

14

DEVIL

My fucking balls ached. They hung blue, heavy, and hurting even though I'd emptied my damn sack a few times a day after finally getting a taste of my woman. Goddamn, just the memory of her tangy sweetness on my tongue, her cum coating my lips, hardened me to the point of pain in a flash.

Too-young pussy, tasty as fuck. The aphrodisiac of the goddamn century.

And she was all mine.

But I had to stay the fuck away from her, or I was in trouble. Keeping my dick inside my jeans while touching and tasting my woman had been the hardest temptation I'd ever faced. Ever. And that's saying something considering all the dirt I had on Hollywood elites and politicians alike.

Me: **I'm taking you for a ride on Saturday.**

I'd planned on a hell of a lot more than that, and riding in various ways.

Jail Bait: **Where we going?**

Me: **North.**

I watched her sitting in the chop shop's office through my monitor, fighting the urge to palm my dick.

Ryker strode into the office, and she dropped her cell into her bag like the damn thing burned her hands. They chatted a bit, he showed her the papers in his hands, and he left once more through the door leading into the shop.

She waited all of two seconds before grabbing her cell again, hunching over it, her fingers flying.

Jail Bait: **Ryker might have a thing or ten to say about that.**

I scowled, knowing she was right—and that I needed to get shit done.

Me: **You let me worry about him.**

Jail Bait: **Pia is making me brownies for after dinner. Want to join us?"**

She nibbled on her lower lip while I debated.

Me: **Rain check on those brownies. I'll pick you up at seven. Dress warm.**

A frown furrowed her brow as she sat back and stared at her phone as though trying to figure out what I had planned.

She'd asked a half-dozen times already every time we'd texted in the previous three days, but I refused to speak up.

I'd thought of stealing her away for the entire damn weekend, locking us away in a motel somewhere Ryker wouldn't find us, but I wanted to make her birthday special and not just about fucking.

Jail Bait: **We're taking the bike?**

I laughed.

Me: **Yes. I'm taking you out for a night on the town—on the back of my bike.**

She did a little dance on the office chair, enough to jiggle her tits.

I bit back a groan and dialed her up even though I'd told myself I wasn't going to talk to her in person until Saturday.

"Hey," she answered, all breathless, twitching my dick hard enough pre-cum oozed from the slit.

"Hey, back." Refusing to be an absolute perv, I clicked off the monitor and closed my eyes, leaning my head back against my chair.

"Why are you calling me at work?" she half-whispered.

"Because I can't stop thinking about you and I'm hard as fuck."

"O-oh." She let out a light giggle, and I shoved my hand beneath my sweats' waist band to grasp my aching length. "Are you going to do anything about it?" she whispered.

"I've already got my hand wrapped around my dick, Jail Bait," I told her, sliding my grip to the base. "Does that make you wet?"

Another puff of laughter sounded in my ear, but more embarrassed than humorous.

I gathered the beading pre-cum and slid back down, imaging it was her pussy grasping at my dick. "Well?"

"Yeah."

"Yeah, what?"

"Knowing you're playing with yourself while talking to me turns me on."

Playing with myself. I bit back my own snort of laughter. There was definitely no playing going on. I shoved my hips upward, groaning at the need tingling in my balls.

"I've been jerking off three times a day," I told her through clenched teeth. Hell, I'd jerked off more in one week than I had my whole damn life. "Thinking about your mouth. Your too-young pussy. Your sweet as fuck ass."

"Will you take that first, too?" she asked, the nervous desire in her voice seizing my balls up tight against my body.

"If you're offering," I groaned out, fighting to keep from blowing my load.

"I want to give that to you," she didn't hesitate to answer—and cum shot up through my dick, spurting all over my t-shirt, sweats, and hand.

"Goddamn, Dasia." I grunted with the last spurt and sank into my chair.

"Did you come?" she whispered.

I glanced at the mess I'd made. "All over the fucking place."

"I wish I was there for another first."

"What's that?" I asked, wiping my sticky hand down my pants.

"Licking it off you."

Fuck. Me. My hand stilled. Could she be any more perfect?

"Gotta go!" she whispered quickly, and the line went dead.

Saturday couldn't come soon enough.

———

I continued to dig through cyberspace, network after network, hacking into home security systems, seeking the shit that would put the entire cartel and Russian mob in the slammer.

The crumb trail I gathered into files took shape, but rather than just dump it all in the FBI's hands, I realized they would need to not just show evidence, but the paths leading to it as well.

When the time came, I would click send on an untraceable email account from an untraceable IP address with the beginnings of that crumb trail. I'd already begun the process so that once sent and opened, the entire trail would flash through, showing exactly what systems I'd hacked.

They just wouldn't know *how*.

Someone banged on my front door, and I pulled up the images from my security system showing the front porch.

Ryker—and the fucker scowled deeper than usual.

Goddamnit.

Heaving a heavy exhale, I pushed up and made my way downstairs.

"What's up, daddy-o?" I asked, pulling the door open.

"If you think you can just make plans to take my girl out without asking, you've got a shit ton of other thinks coming, you cock-sucking prick." Pissiness radiated off his tense shoulders, but he hadn't yet fisted his hands at his sides.

"Want a beer?" I asked, turning and leaving the door open for him.

The door slammed shut before I reached the kitchen, and I bit back a chuckle as his boots stomped toward me.

"I planned on swinging by the shop today to talk to you."

"The fuck you even asking her out for a ride without talking to me *first*?"

I popped one cap and handed it to him, but he shook his head. Shrugging, I put the other away and took a long pull of the cold one I clutched a bit too tightly. He could squash me with his bare hands— but I'd learned a few defensive moves in the previous two weeks of karate class.

"She's going to be eighteen on Saturday, Ryker."

"So?"

"You're not her father."

"Fuck you, Devil. She's under my protection,

living in my goddamn house. Hell, I even hugged the girl last night—the only person other than Pia I can stand to touch."

My eyebrows shot up, and I lowered my beer. I knew he didn't like to be touched, but fuck. "Seriously?"

He glanced away, his throat working—and I found myself face to face with a man I'd never met in the dozen plus years I'd known him.

"You're right. I should have asked first," I said, my voice quiet.

Ryker turned his cold green eyes on my face.

"I'm sorry."

He stared long enough I fought the need to shift on my feet, and stuck his hand out.

I jerked my focus back up to his face.

"You have my permission."

I considered being a cocky jerk and telling him I didn't need his goddamn permission, but grasped his calloused hand instead—for the first time since I'd met him years earlier. "Thanks, Ryker."

His beard twitched as though he clenched his jaw, and I released my hold so he could wipe his palm down his jeans. "You fuck with her heart, and I'll rip yours from your chest with my bare fucking hands."

I held up my hands, bottle neck of my beer in a lighter hold.

"Saturday night," he snipped, nodding. "You can pick her up at seven, but I expect her home by midnight."

Biting back a retort, I nodded. "You got it, daddy-o."

He spun and stomped back the hallway again.

"What changed your mind?" I called after him.

"Turns out I've got a soft as fuck heart for big blue eyes welling with tears!" he barked back without looking at me.

Well, I'll be damned.

The door slammed shut behind him, and I chuckled while lifting my beer to my lips. The callous, cold bastard really had grown a heart.

And little Jail Bait had begged—with tears—to spend the night on the back of my bike.

Goddamn, I was so ready to fucking roll.

My heart stuttered in my chest when Dasia came skipping out Ryker's front door, cheeks pink and eyes sparkling with stars in them.

Ryker and Pia stood behind her on the stoop as I climbed off my bike.

Dasia pulled up abruptly in front of me, her smile dazzling—fucking owning me. Had her adoptive parents, of a sort, not stood behind her, I expect she would have thrown herself into my arms.

I glanced at Ryker. He scowled. I nodded, taking the hint.

"Where're we going?" Dasia asked with that breathless tone that stirred my dick to life.

"It's a surprise." I handed her my extra helmet and helped her clasp it beneath her chin, the long braid of her red hair laying over her chest giving me all kinds of kinky thoughts.

Later.

Grinning, I tapped her helmet. "Let's ride."

"Enjoy your freedom!" Pia called from the porch, and Dasia climbed on behind me, her laughter fucking music to my ears.

Her arms went around me, the heat of her front, the softness of her tits crushed against my back enough to make me hard—and groan.

Patience, I told my dick and roared the engine to life.

I shot up Route 1, heading north into New Hampshire. Dasia clung to me, and I'd never been happier in my goddamn life. Open road, whipping, mild wind, and a warm palm sneaking beneath my sweatshirt.

The girl was going to drive me fucking insane. Temptation to bypass my plans to sip hot chocolate while sitting at Hampton Beach had me eyeing every motel we passed.

I'd promised to take her out, though, and I wasn't one to fail or go back on my word.

I slowed and pulled into a parking spot along the ocean wall, glad to find the bulk of tourists had dwindled with the heat of summer giving way to cooler temps. At least my favorite shop still sat open.

Dasia eyed me while I helped her with the helmet clasp, but rather than explain where I'd brought her, I entwined my fingers through hers and dragged her across the street.

"They have the best hot chocolate," I told her as we pulled up in front of the coffee shop's to-go window.

Five minutes later, we sat on a bench, watching the waves out in the distance. A salt-scented breeze blew in off the ocean, but not enough to chill us the fuck through—especially since we held steaming cups of rich hot chocolate.

People trickled by on the walkway in front of us as we sat thigh to thigh.

"So, what's it feel like to be eighteen?"

She laughed again, and the sheer joy emanating off her gave me a high unlike any I'd known.

"You have no idea how *free* I feel right now. I've been counting down the days for years." Her smile faded as a bigger wave crashed on shore and a gull swooped in to land at our feet, his beady eyes watching us in hopes we dropped a tasty morsel for him to snatch up.

I kicked at the damn thing, and he took to flight again with a sharp cry as a guy in khakis strolled past, hands shoved in his pockets and shoulders hunched.

"What are your plans now that you've got that freedom you've been longing for?" I asked.

She shrugged and turned to face me, her smile gone, but eyes still happy. "Until I know I'm really free to move about how and when I please, I'm not making any."

"You mean the whole Ivan affair."

"Yeah." She sipped, searching my face.

"I'm almost there," I told her with finality in my tone. "I promise I'm going to set you free."

Dasia turned away toward the ocean once more,

but not before I caught the disappointment in her eyes. If she thought I planned on setting her free of me, she was in for one hell of a surprise.

"I can't call you Jail Bait anymore."

She huffed a light laugh without the joy from earlier. "I *am* legal now."

Thank fuck. "How about I call you my sweet little pussy cat instead?"

She shot me a quick glance and raised eyebrow.

"What part don't you like?" I asked. "The *pussy* or *my* part?"

Pink fused her cheeks. "You're serious about being broken together, aren't you?"

"Dead fucking serious, Dasia. The first time I saw you at the gate, the pulling in my gut..." I had to swallow against a rush of emotion I couldn't name. "Fucking beat to hell and shivering—bruised and yet a hint of fire in your eyes—you owned me. Couldn't look away even though the sight of your battered body filled me with rage."

"You were so gentle," she whispered.

"I wanted to tear into the person who hurt you —still do."

The man in khaki's strolled past in my periphery again, and I glanced up to find him jerking his focus off us to the cell in his hand. My nape tingled, and I kept my attention on him as he moved off a little ways and leaned against a light post.

"Adrian?"

"Do you recognize that guy?" I asked, motioning with my head, my stomach turning hard.

She turned to look. "No."

Once her focus returned to my face, I forced my own off the guy even though I couldn't rid myself of a feeling of wrongness. I scanned the area around us, noting his quickly glancing back down when I turned his way once more.

A muscle ticked in my jaw, but he moved off a few seconds later.

My stomach refused to rest. "Come on," I said, standing and reaching for her hand. We ambled back toward the bike, finishing off our drinks and tossing them into a can.

On alert yet not wanting to worry Dasia, I forced myself to take my time while hooking her helmet. Unable to help myself, I laid a kiss on the tip of her nose.

"Where are we heading now?" she asked, her smile returning.

I considered the ride I had planned and going with my gut feeling, I changed my mind. "Time to go get your present," I told her, and turned to climb on my bike, taking a quick scan of our surroundings while doing so.

The bike roared to life, and Dasia climbed on, hugging my back in the best fucking way possible.

Khaki prick wasn't anywhere that I could see—but after getting on the highway once more and making a few turns, I expected he drove the dark sedan following us.

I clasped over Dasia's hand beneath my sweatshirt resting on my abs. "Gonna open it up. Hang on!"

She let out a squeal of laughter as I shot forward, weaving onto Route 95 south. The wind whipped, the engine of my orange baby tearing it the fuck up.

I considered my place rather than getting her back to the safety of Ryker's, but wondered how much we'd been compromised. Taking her to the club might not be safe, either.

We needed to disappear until I could straighten shit out.

Losing the dark sedan in my side mirror took less than a mile even though the fucker had sped up trying to keep within sight of our asses. I took the next exit and headed west, my focus split between the road ahead and my rear view mirrors.

Once sure no one followed, my stomach eased

up a bit, and even though I knew I had a call to make, my body took interest in Dasia's warm hands on my stomach, her pinkies shoved into my jeans' waistband, and where we headed.

And I'd thought her cheeks were pink earlier. She pulled off the helmet before I could help, her gaze flitting over the big brick building I'd parked behind. "I don't suppose we're here for dinner, are we?"

"No." I clasped her hand in mine, and she willingly strode by my side into the inn. I paid cash at the wood-paneled desk, only letting go of her hand when signing for the room.

We headed up the stairs with their old fashioned wooden railing, the thick carpet hushing our footsteps even as we rounded the landing to the second floor. My heart thumped heavy in my chest, but more than from the thought of finally getting her naked in my arms.

I let us into the room, locking and bolting the door behind me.

"What's this?" she asked, biting back a smile while turning toward me.

Fighting to keep my concern to myself, I spread my arms wide. "Your present."

She narrowed her gaze but with a playfulness that twitched my dick. "*You're* my present?"

"I'm all the present you'll ever need, pussy cat."

A snorted laugh escaped her. "Has anyone told you you're arrogant as hell?"

"Yep, as well I should be."

She set her hands on her hips and slowly slid her gaze down over me, hardening my dick fully. "I think you'll do." Her breathless tone clued me in to her nervousness even though she acted calm and sassy.

I considered stalking toward her and *showing* her I would do just fucking fine, but I had a phone call to make first. Sitting in the closest chair, I eyed the bathroom, ready to drop a lie to get a moment's privacy.

She took a quick inhale as I shucked my first boot as though realizing I meant business—and what we were about to do.

"I'll be right out," she squeaked, disappearing into the bathroom and locking the door before I could tell her I needed to head in there myself.

Quick as fuck, I pulled out my cell and moved to the other end of the room, cuffing my mouth with my hand as Ryker answered.

"Ryker—we had a tail," I rushed to say. "Not sure

who the fuck it is, and Dasia didn't recognize him either."

"Where are you?"

"At an inn in Exeter."

"She okay?"

I glanced at the closed bathroom door. "I don't think she even knows we were followed," I whispered.

"Good. You stay put. I'll call Vigil. And Devil?"

"Yeah?"

"Take it easy on that girl, you hear me?"

I grinned, my dick still on board. "I'm not going to do anything she doesn't consent to."

"Better not, you sick fuck."

The sink's water turned on, and I tossed my cell onto the bed stand, putting aside thoughts of what waited outside our room, the threat of unknown fuckers wanting to find her.

Time to focus on making my pussy cat purr in pleasure.

15

DASIA

I stared at myself in the mirror as the rush of water flushed the toilet behind me.

I'm eighteen now. Free, I told myself, trying to calm the mad swarm of butterflies in my stomach.

I hadn't really expected Adrian to bring me to a hotel, but I'd definitely hoped for something along those lines. His low tone sounded out in the room as I inhaled a steadying breath while ripping the tiny bar of soap open.

Warm water rushed from the spigot as I washed my hands slowly, taking time to fight off my nervousness.

I'd made a shit ton of bad decisions in the past couple of months that landed me in trouble, but something inside me knew Adrian—Devil—wasn't a bad choice. He'd kept his dick in his pants while wanting to get into mine, waited for me to be of legal age. A horny asshole would have taken me willingly that night we sat outside on Ryker's back patio because God knew I'd been more than willing.

He hadn't, and because of it, I trusted him.

I huffed a snort while drying my hands on a fluffy white towel that smelled heavily of bleach.

Ryker trusted him, otherwise he never would have allowed me to head off on his Harley. I trusted Pia. Pia trusted Ryker who trusted Devil. Yet another reason I knew he wasn't a bad choice.

But could I give up control and submit fully to what he wanted?

Getting involved meant a possible break up, and I considered fucking him just to get a taste of what my body craved, but driving him away to protect my heart afterward wasn't what I truly wanted.

I wouldn't hook up with him just to keep from being lonely, though. With him, I didn't feel lost or alone. He and I connected in ways I never had with anyone, not even my best friend Stacey. Like me, he didn't trust easily, and also like me, he wanted to be in control to keep from being hurt again.

That is what drew me to him. That is why I

wanted to know him better. That was why I wanted him.

I want this.

He'd shown me vulnerability, trust when I hadn't yet earned it, and I was ready to give him mine.

One last exhale, and I grasped the bathroom door handle, my heart in my throat.

Adrian sprawled on the chair, legs spread, his palms resting on the ends of the arm rests. He ensnared me with those bedroom eyes, and my body came alive as he slid his gaze down over me while I stood like a deer in the headlights in the bathroom doorway.

"Come here." That raspy, low timbre slid down over my body like a caress, and I moved on auto pilot, his voice commanding my brain waves. My nipples pebbled tight, and wetness from his intense gaze alone soaked clear through my panties.

"Stop," he whispered when I stood less than two feet from his knees.

My feet halted.

"Would you strip for me?"

I let out an audible gulp, but far from one of fear. Stripping had been a bad choice, but hell if I wanted to say no to Adrian. Letting out a slow, steady exhale through my nose, I turned and bent at the waist, all but shoving my ass in his face.

"Goddamn," he groaned, and I bit back my smirk while my shaking fingers unzipped my boots.

Once unzipped, I bent my knees and slowly slid back to a stand, gyrating my hips enough to pull another groan from him. I slid my feet free and turned, hands on my jean's button while moving as though music slammed into my ears rather than our heavy breaths.

Adrian's focus zoned in on my fingers as I unsnapped and unzipped my jeans. Another turn and side-to-side shimmying of my hips lowered the jeans to my knees, and low curses escaped him as I slid them to the floor, my satin-covered ass once more in his face.

My hands still shook, but I managed to rid myself of my socks without breaking from the seductive movements. A glance over my shoulder once standing showed him drooling over the ass I'd always thought too big, too juicy. He looked like he wanted to take a big bite, and the thought of his mouth on me sent another rush of arousal to my panties.

I gathered up my sweatshirt and long-sleeve t-shirt in my hands, and pulled them off overhead, baring my back. They swished to the floor, and I continued to move my hips while reaching behind me to unsnap my bra.

My breasts ached, and I caught their weight as the bra sagged—slowly turning to slip one arm free, then the other.

"Let me see your tits, pussy cat," he rasped, his tone stroking over me like a flame, his white-knuckled grip on the arm rests revealing his restraint. His control.

I dropped my bra and held my breasts, squeezing my thighs together while continuing to dance.

Rather than close my eyes and getting lost in the music like I'd done at the strip club, I kept my focus on him while feeling myself up—taking my arousal to another level.

"Fuck, Dasia." He swallowed, his focus sliding down to my soaked panties. "Take them off and get on the bed."

I turned and sashayed away, giving an extra sway to my hips and paused at the bed's foot to shimmy the soaked panties off my body. Another groan from him, and I climbed atop the bed he'd turned down, keeping my ass in the air while glancing over my shoulder.

He stood and stalked forward like an animal

after prey, but I was a willing victim. I wanted to be pounced upon. Devoured. All trace of aversion had disappeared over the past couple of days—when, I didn't know for sure, but relief over that war having been won set me free to enjoy my birthday gift.

I turned and lowered my ass to the bed, reaching for the long braid over my shoulder, intending to set the fiery strands he loved free.

"Don't."

I obeyed and leaned back on my hands, jutting my breasts toward him. A slow slide of my feet toward my ass set my heels on the mattress—and gave him an unhindered view of my pussy.

He ripped his shirt off overhead, and I nearly swooned. Absolute perfection—tanned skin, thick pecs, and rippled abs ... that luscious V dipping into jeans he grasped himself through.

A few strokes over his jeans, and he shoved them down, springing his cock free. Thick and long.

I gulped even though my pussy spasmed at the thought of being stuffed full.

Would it hurt? My first time had, but I hadn't been prepared—hadn't wanted it.

Fuck. Did I really want another dick inside my body?

I blinked and jerked my focus up to his face to find him staring at me.

"You okay?" he whispered, his entire body tensed to spring.

"I-I don't know."

"Lay back, pussy cat."

I did as told, my gaze glued to his face as he crawled onto the bed, resting on his haunches between my bent legs. Holding my gaze, he caressed the tops of my feet, up my shins, to rest his palms on my knees.

"We don't have to do this," he told me, his thumbs rubbing in small circles on the insides of my knees. "Tell me no, and I'll just hold you."

"I-I want to," I told him, telling myself I did, too.

He leaned down over me, his hands by my shoulders, his brown eyes soft even though lust stroked the fire to life inside me again, tensing me beneath him. "You're in charge, Dasia, understand? I want this to be good for you, I won't push you."

Swallowing, I nodded, my hands grasping hold of his hard forearms. Muscle flexed beneath my hold.

"Come here." He lowered himself, wrapped his arms around me, and turned all in a single motion, pulling me atop him.

I straddled his thighs, the wetness from my pussy smearing over the back of his cock. Holding my gaze, he interlocked his fingers behind his head, showing off the flexed muscles of his biceps.

God...

Fucking perfect.

I leaned forward to trace my fingertips over his perfectly arched eyebrows, down his nose—over his hot as fuck mouth with its sensual curve. Along his clean-shaven jaw, down over his throat and the bobbing apple inside.

Hard pecs, soft skin—not a single hair on his chest, thank God. Tight nipples...

I bent down fully and nipped my teeth over one, and he jolted beneath me, his cock sliding along my slit and rubbing my throbbing clit.

My breath left in a rush, and I sat back up, my hands on his abs, my eyes wide.

He thrust again, coating the back of his cock with my arousal, but not hitting my clit. I leaned down, my hands beside his chest.

"Do that again," I whispered, damn near drowning in his amber eyes.

He gyrated beneath me, his length rubbing over my clit, and my eyelids fluttered shut as a shudder rippled through me.

I want him—want this.

I opened my eyes. "I want you, Adrian."

"Then sheath me up and take me, pussy cat."

"Wha—"

"Condom," he said, releasing his hands to point at the bed stand with his thumb.

Oh.

I grabbed the foil packet he must have placed there, my trust in him settling deeper into my soul. Had he told me to take him, I would have without a thought of protection and pregnancy.

Stupid.

I fumbled with the damn thing, and he grasped my shaking hands.

"Dasia?"

I let out a slow breath and relaxed, handing the packet to him. "You do it."

I scooted back off his hips, my focus dropping to his cock and the droplet of moisture beaded at the slit. Without a thought, I leaned down and licked, the salty musk of him flooding my mouth with drool.

He cursed through clenched teeth, and I licked again, getting a taste of myself in the process. Someday I would give him that first, but I needed him inside me.

Straightening, I wanted to tell him to hurry as he

pulled out the condom and slowly rolled the damn thing down over his straining length. The second he shoved his hands behind his head, I slid forward, past the tip of his cock until it sprang back up to tap against my ass.

I'll give him that first one day—but not today.

Lifting to a plank, I reached between us and grasped his thick girth.

He groaned as I notched the tip inside me.

I paused, his cock barely inside me, my hands grasping at the sheets beside his pecs, our gazes locked, my lips parted. His arms flexed as his entire body tensed beneath me.

"Dasia," he whispered through gritted teeth as though teetering on the edge of his control. One thrust of his hips would bury him inside my soaked channel, but he held still—shaking beneath me.

I slowly pressed back onto him, his girth stretching me, filling me to the point of discomfort.

I'm soaking wet—I want him. I can take him.

Clenching my own jaw, I shoved back, stuffing myself full.

"Fuck." He closed his eyes, his head tipping back, veins popping along his neck and forehead. "Fuck, baby."

"Touch me," I whispered, my heart in my throat,

the tip of his cock so far deep inside me, I felt he'd pierced my heart.

Opening his eyes, he grasped my hips, slowly sliding me forward along his length.

I groaned when he flexed his hips while pushing me back onto his cock again. Three slow thrusts spiraled my thoughts to heaven and back again. I rode a gentle wave of building euphoria as his hard length dragged against my grasping inner walls.

He buried deep and gyrated his hips.

"God," I gasped as he rubbed against my cervix. "Oh, God."

With a groan, he grabbed hold of my braid and tugged me down against his chest. "I'm the devil," he growled and took my mouth with a bruising kiss.

I cried out as he slammed into me. My pussy tingled, my clit sliding harshly against his lower abs as he fucked into me over and over, the fullness ... the lingering taste of chocolate on his tongue ... the sweet scent of licorice and sex filling my nose.

He released my hair and snaked his hand between us.

"Come all over my cock, pussy cat—milk me dry."

A pinch to my clit sent me shrieking over the edge of reality, and hard arms banded around me, holding me as I convulsed with every spasm of my pussy, his own grunts and curses prolonging my climax.

His cock swelled incredibly thicker, and he jerked beneath me, buried so deep inside me, it bordered on pain—but the best kind.

"Fuck, Dasia." He pulled out and slammed back in with another grunt, and a shiver slid down my spine as I opened my eyes to watch the rest of his climax play out on his face.

He had his eyes open and locked on mine. Lower lip between his teeth. Nostrils flared, eyes filled with so much damn emotion my chest ached. Another thrust and he stilled, his teeth releasing his lip.

"Come here," he rasped.

I closed the distance between us and had my first ever after sex kiss—and it couldn't have been more perfect, full of emotion, of promise.

Yeah. The devil had definitely given me the best present ever.

16

DEVIL

We shared a pillow, our bodies entwined from chest to toes. Best pillow talk of my life. She had me laughing and groaning for more, the little kinky vixen.

"Seriously." she said, her eyes alight. "I didn't think you were going to fit."

I nudged my nose against hers. "You were a slick, sloppy mess. No way in hell I wouldn't."

Another sweet kiss, the softness of her mouth driving me fucking insane. I would never get enough of touching her. Tasting her. Ever.

"So, now that you've had me, plan on setting me free?"

"Fuck no," I grumbled, tightening my arms around her. "You're not getting rid of me."

I pulled back enough to take in her sleepy eyes, the smear of mascara beneath, and the satisfied, relaxed smile on her lips.

"You're so damn beautiful." I brushed her hair off her brow, lifting the long tresses I'd unbraided and run my fingers through an hour after cleaning up the mess we'd made between her thighs. I held the handful of hair to my nose and breathed in the sweet springtime, fresh and flowery. "Smell damn good, too."

Her smile widened, the pulse in her neck picking up speed.

I hadn't been too rough with her, but with it only being her second time and me packing some girth, I wasn't about to rush things and make her regret allowing me between her legs.

We had time.

My cell rang, and I kissed her forehead before rolling away with a groan.

Vigil.

"I gotta take this, okay?"

Dasia nodded back at me, and I swiped to answer while walking toward the bathroom, her "Nice ass!" whisper holler making me grin.

"What's up?" I asked Vigil.

"Stone and Greed will meet you at your house in

the morning," Vigil said as I shut myself into the bathroom. "I want you to gather up all the shit you've compiled—I know it's not as much as you wanted, but we need to get this boat rolling. Think they can at least get arrest warrants with what you've got so far?"

"Shit, yeah."

"Okay. Get to the club tomorrow at nine."

"You gonna tell Ryker we're spending the night here so I don't have to hear his shit?"

"He's the one who told me to tell you to stay rather than drag her ass here to the club at this time of night."

I knew it ran close to midnight. "Thanks, Vigil."

"See you in the a.m."

I hung up, took care of business since I was already in the bathroom, and returned to find Dasia's eyes closed, her hands beneath her cheek. She peeled up an eyelid to peek at me as I slid beneath the blankets and tucked my body against hers.

"Sleep, pussy cat," I whispered against her forehead. "Ryker knows I'm keeping you tonight."

She smiled and drifted off while I considered the next night and the next and the next. I'd had a taste, but my hunger for her hadn't even begun to be satisfied. I hoped once the shit of our circumstances settled the fuck down, I could talk her into staying. Forever.

But would the young, newly freed woman want my old ass? I didn't have a single gray hair yet. Sure, I had a line or two by my eyes from smiling too damn much, but my body looked better than it had at twenty.

Fucking get over yourself, I told myself, shutting my eyes. If she wanted to go, I would make myself let her—because I cared about her more than my own selfish desires.

Maybe if I got lucky, she'd see that and eventually come back.

———

We had breakfast in bed, and even though I'd woken with a raging hard on, I kept from climbing aboard her like I wanted to. That didn't stop me from taking a shower with her and scrubbing every inch of her body and playing with that little clit while my mouth was full of tit until she came undone in my arms.

She insisted on returning the favor, so I soaped up my dick and showed her what to do. Tentative at first, she got the hang—and the proper grip—and got me off faster than I could myself.

Goddamn, did she get my wheels going.

We took off southward, but not until I'd carefully scoped around the small parking lot without her catching on. No need to get her fear going until the last possible minute.

The ride south stirred my dick again thanks to Dasia's wandering hands, but the sight of Stone's truck in my driveway and him and Greed, Warden's other security officer, sitting in the cab, killed it. They climbed from the truck as I rumbled to a stop in front of my garage door.

"Hey!" Dasia called to Stone while climbing off my bike and unhooking her helmet. "What are you doing here?"

Stone caught my eye and raised an eyebrow.

I shook my head.

"I'll fill you in once we're inside," he told Dasia while Greed scanned my neighborhood, standing at a seemingly relaxed pose, but he'd been trained by both Warden and Stone. The boy might not be bigger than me, but he could throw down.

"Dasia, this is Greed. Greed, this is my girl Dasia."

Dasia beamed at him, her cheeks flushing.

"Hey, sweet thing," Greed said, his pretty boy smile flashing back at her as he clasped her hand. "Seen you around ... sorry I haven't had a chance to meet you yet."

"Well, with the way Ryker hovers, that's no big surprise," she told him with a light laugh.

Greed glanced at me. "And with this fucker claiming you, you won't have a lick of freedom left."

Dasia's smile faltered, and I entwined my fingers with hers. "She's free to do whatever the fuck she wants," I forced myself to say, even though it felt like a knife slashed through my chest. "Come on. The bike ride was kind of cold. You gotta be freezing."

She shrugged and nodded, and I tugged her toward the covered porch leading to my front door.

I'd had the place built in the hopes of maybe someday finding a woman who I could trust with my vulnerability. It came easy with Dasia, even knowing she could easily walk away once the threat cleared up, taking my heart along with her.

My heart.

Yeah. I was fucking done for.

Waking to her face inches from mine, blue eyes clear and peering at me—that damn emotion I'd never felt before ached through my chest, and I'd named it for what it was, just not out loud. Too soon for that shit, and I didn't want to give her anything more to have to think on. She'd have enough once I told her why Stone and Greed met us at my house.

I gave her a quick tour of the first floor, decent sized kitchen for my chef-wannabe ass, the man cave living room with its huge ass TV dominating almost an entire wall, and the small bath and laundry room adjacent.

Motioning with my head to the living room for Stone and Greed to make themselves comfortable, I started for the stairs.

"Go on," I told Dasia, grinning as she obeyed and I followed her ass up the stairs, every sway of her hips twitching my dick again.

Couldn't fucking wait to bury my entire length between those plump cheeks—have the life squeezed from my dick by her virgin hole...

I adjusted myself while stepping onto the landing, and pulled her left into my room.

"Bedroom. Master bath," I said, motioning toward the far door, "and that's the walk-in closet I promised."

"Mmm." She smiled at me, but I turned and pulled her back out of the master suite before either of us got any fun ideas.

"Guest room," I said, pointing at the door on the

right even though it didn't have a damn thing in it. "Guest bathroom." Another thumb toward the next door. "And this," I pushed open the door at the back of the hallway, "is my office."

The damn room was just as big as my master suite and was jammed full of shit most people wouldn't know what to do with. It was the large half-circle desk that Dasia moved toward, her head moving side to side while taking in my monitors. Some ran non-stop, jumping from one camera to another while the security system kept watch over my two and a half acre lot.

"This is incredible," she said quietly, stopping at my chair and putting her hands on the top. "Did you build all this?"

"Pretty much." I stepped up beside her, watching her face as she took everything in. "How do you even ... shit, I can't even handle a damn cell phone's technology." She laughed and turned toward me. "You're a real-life geek."

"Told you so."

I sat and pulled her sideways onto my lap. "I want to show you something."

A few clicks brought up my encrypted email with its bread crumb trail I'd mostly finished up the morning before while waiting to pick Dasia up after her birthday dinner with Pia and Ryker.

I clicked the email onto the bigger screen to the right and swiveled to face it.

Dasia slowly straightened while reading, her eyes widening. "Holy..."

I waited for her to reach the bottom of the screen.

"Is that ... *the* Ivan?"

"His real name is Alexi Dvornikov, and he's the head of a sex slave operation in Boston for the Russian mafia."

"Oh, God." She stared at his name. "I really would have been sold as a sex slave."

"Yeah."

A shiver wracked through her, and I wrapped my arms around her, pulling her tight against my chest.

"That man at the ocean yesterday," I said, hating to freak her out but needing to, "you're sure you didn't recognize him?"

"No."

I sat quiet and used one hand to pull up a file I planned to attach to the email bound for the FBI.

She kept her body tight to mine, but shifted to watch as I scrolled through the images, some blurred a bit, but most clear as day.

Khaki man made an appearance alongside Alexi Dvornikov in a picture the FBI had on file.

"That's him," I said without a doubt in my head.

"Oh, God. Did you know?"

"Not until just now, but I had a weird vibe when he walked past us the second time."

"That's why we left so abruptly, isn't it?" Dasia asked, turning her focus on me.

"Yeah. It's also why I sped down the highway—we had a tail for close to a mile before I smoked his ass."

I sat staring at the fucker before it hit me. "How did he know where to find you? Did you tell anyone where you were?"

"The only one I talked to outside the club since getting here is Stacey."

"Did you tell her where you were?"

"No."

"Did you say *anything* that would hint at your being here?"

She chewed on her lower lip but shook her head. "I'm positive—at least I'm pretty sure."

"Call her."

Dasia pulled out her cell and called, but it went straight to voicemail. "Hey, Stacey, it's me. Give me a call when you get this." She hung up, her hands shaking. "You don't think..."

Another tremble swept over her, and I leaned back in my chair, pulling her in tight again, my lips on the top of her head. "At this point, I don't know what to think, but we're sending all this shit I got on those boys into the FBI, Dasia. Hopefully, in a few days we'll start hearing of arrests."

"And until then?" she whispered, fear evident in her shaking voice.

"Until then, you and I are heading into the club, and we'll keep trying to get in touch with your friend. Vigil wants to meet with all the officers and make a final decision on anonymously handing this compiled evidence over."

Dasia pulled back and searched my face. "This is what you've been doing since you met me, isn't it? Hacking and..." She waved her hand at my desk.

"Yeah."

"Why? What do you stand to gain?"

"Your safety." I tucked some of the hair that escaped her braid behind her ear. "Your freedom."

Her lower lip trembled as she peered at me, tears welling in her eyes. "You didn't even know me."

"Something inside me knew you the second I saw you at the Vipers' gate, Dasia. Knew you were meant to be in my life. I promised I would keep you safe, and I meant it."

Tears slid down her cheeks as she leaned forward and pressed her lips softly against mine. "Thank you."

"I'd do anything for you, pussy cat. Surely you must know that by now."

Another kiss—and another.

Ten minutes passed before she climbed off my lap and I gave her ass a gentle swat. "Let me get my shit together, then we're heading to the club."

17

DASIA

Ryker and Pia hadn't arrived at the club by the time we got there. A woman I'd seen at the two parties came out of the kitchen area with a big plate of bacon and a carton of orange juice. A stack of plates and plastic forks sat on the unmanned bar's edge.

"Hey, Devil," she said with a smirk before checking me out real quick as I moved alongside him, her smile fading a little bit.

"Tina, have you met Dasia?" Adrian asked her.

"No, but I've seen her around." She snipped the words but set the bacon on the bar and came over, offering her hand. "Don't worry," she said, glancing at Adrian again before turning back to me, "I won't try to steal your man."

"My man?" A light laugh escaped me, but neither one of them smiled.

"I'm a club whore," she said, and I stared, processing. "And I swear there's something in the air lately, all these brothers finding their old ladies. Fuck." She propped her hands on her hips, lips pressing in a tight line for a few seconds before turning away. "I'm making a mess of pancakes for all your horny asses!" she called before disappearing into the kitchen again.

Adrian chuckled and tugged me toward the office door which stood open.

"Hey, little girl," Vigil said when we walked in after Adrian knocked on the door jam. "His ass treating you good?"

Heat flushed my face, and I shoved my hands in my jeans' pockets with a shrug as Adrian released my hand to put his computer bag on Vigil's desk. "Yeah. He's doing alright."

"Alright?" Vigil barked a laugh, his wide shoulders shaking and pale eyes actually showing a bit of humor for the first time since I'd met him. "If he's only doing alright, you ought to think about finding yourself a real man."

"Vigil." Adrian's tone came out low—almost a

growl, jerking my focus toward him. He glared at his club's president, hands fisting at his sides.

"Cool your ass, boy," Vigil said with a chuckle, motioning toward a shabby couch to our left. "Sit down and relax, little girl. Everyone else is running late."

"Stone's outside with Greed."

The front door slammed, and Tina's purr and Greed's, "Hey, sweet thing" floated through the office door we'd left open.

Vigil rolled his eyes. "Fucker ought to just claim the woman and get it over with. Damn woman has been salivating over him ever since Shaun took Warden off the market."

I glanced at Adrian.

"Might have been some jealousy there," he said with a wink. "Go on. Sit. I'm going to get my shit out."

I sat, keeping my hands from touching the filthy, rough-looking material stretched thin over the old couch. God knew how much bodily fluids that thing had ground into it.

Stone sauntered in and took one of the chairs in front of Vigil's desk. Adrian finally took the other, scooting close to Vigil's desk where he'd set up his laptop. He clicked away while Vigil and Stone bullshitted for a few minutes—and heavy clomps sounded outside the door.

"'Bout fucking time you get your lazy ass down here," Vigil told his brother.

Ricky flicked him off and slumped into a chair against the wall, his eyes bleary. He nodded at me, but didn't speak a word. While not as big as his brother, the two could have easily passed for twins with their reddish hair and blue eyes.

I texted Stacey and waited a few minutes before shoving my cell back in my pocket again, nerves like piranhas eating away at my stomach.

The front door opened out in the club, and the sound of Pia's voice eased some of the tension in my shoulders. Finally, another woman. She laughed, and someone answered—Giada, I recognized her voice, too.

Ryker filled the office doorway, his gaze swinging to find me. "Dasia."

He didn't toss out a question, but I'd gotten to know him enough to see it in his cold eyes.

I smiled and nodded, letting him know I was just fine.

"Why don't you head on out with Pia and have some breakfast while the men chat," he said.

I hopped up, happy to be off the gross couch, and

gave him a real quick hug before scuttling past. "Thanks, Ryk."

Vigil chuckled and mumbled something about "softie" but I shut the door behind me so as not to embarrass my friend.

Pia eyed me as I hurried toward her sitting at the bar's end in front of the bacon. "How are you?" she asked, sliding off the stool to hug me.

"Good." I hugged her tight, loving how her arms felt like what I imagined a real mom did. "Doing really good."

She held me at arm's length and studied my face. Giada sitting on her other side laughed around a mouthful of bacon. "I wondered if that pretty boy geek was any good in bed," she said. "Your face says it all."

"Oh, come on!" Greed said from a few stools away where he shoveled pancakes into his mouth. "I'm trying to eat over here!"

Heat flooded up my face, and Pia shushed Giada while gesturing for me to sit.

"Spill," Giada whispered at the same time Pia asked me about my night.

I wasn't about to give details to a woman I hardly knew and another I considered more a mom than friend, never mind the cute Viper brother within ear shot. Sticking to the details—bike ride, hot chocolate, staying a night at the inn, driving back in the freaking cold morning, having to sit on Vigil's couch —only earned me a couple of frowns.

"Tight lipped little bitch," Giada said while smiling. "We aren't going to get shit out of you, are we?"

I shook my head, grabbed a piece of cold bacon, and shoved it into my mouth.

"At least tell us if he's as big as the rumors?"

A bit of bacon went down the wrong tube, and I coughed as Greed shot to his feet. "That's it, I'm out!" he strolled through to the kitchen where Tina's purr greeted him.

"Well?" Giada pressed.

"Well what?" I feigned innocence.

"Bitch," Giada said with a laugh.

Even though a pile of shit surrounded my life, caused a mess outside the club, I found myself completely at ease. Even when Tina came out of the kitchen with Greed in tow to join us a half hour or so later, both flushed and hair mussed, I felt accepted.

Had the whore ridden Adrian's dick? Probably. The thought irked me, but that was the past, I told myself, and we had a future. Besides, she was all over Greed, her legs propped across his and rubbing against the bulge in his leathers.

"Probably should have waited to make all this until after church," Tina muttered, eyeing the stack of pancakes she'd brought out on a sheet pan.

"Church?" I asked while pouring myself some orange juice.

"That." Tina pointed over her shoulder at the closed office door. "The officers meeting."

Pia shrugged when I glanced her way. "I don't get it."

I imagined what Adrian thought of using that word for their meetings, but shrugged it off. It obviously didn't bother him enough to make him want to skip out.

18

DEVIL

"I put together a nice little breadcrumb trail," I tried explaining for the second time.

"Why the fuck didn't you just toss all the evidence into one email?" Ryker asked, arms crossed and scowling from where he stood leaning against the office wall.

"Just trying to make sure none of this shit can come up as inadmissible in court. It's gotta be authentic."

"They're the fucking FBI," Ryker argued. "They can pretty much do anything. No goddamn court will argue with them if they don't want 'em to."

"If that was the case," Ricky muttered from his chair, eyes closed and head tipped back against the wall, "then they wouldn't even need this evidence, now, would they?"

"Just send it," Vigil said, his tone firm. "Let's get this fucking ball rolling."

I hit the send button, the tension in my shoulders lessening enough I felt I could breathe easier. "Done."

"Dasia is staying at the club until this shit is over," Vigil said, his stare on me.

"Then I'm staying, too." The side of my face burned beneath Ryker's stare. I turned to find him scowling at me exactly as I'd expected. "Something on your mind?"

His beard twitched as though he clenched his jaw.

"She's mine," I stated with zero question in my head, heart, or voice. "Mine to protect, mine to fuck. And I won't share, either." I glanced at Ricky since we'd done that very thing a time or two. "Anyone touches her, and they're dead."

"She's a little young," Vigil said, drawing my focus off his brother who ignored me.

"Fuck you."

He chuckled but slapped his palm on his desk. "Devil is claiming Dasia. Anyone got a problem with that?" Turning toward Ryker, he lifted an eyebrow, and I did the same.

Ryker kept his glare on me rather than our president. I would fight whoever thought to keep me from her and wasn't about to back down to his scary as hell scowl.

The fucker nodded.

I heaved an exhale at having his blessing I'd never expected to get. Yeah, he'd given permission for me to take her on the back of my bike, but to claim the young woman? Hell, no.

"You've got security on his house?" Vigil asked me, pulling me back to business.

"He doesn't have jack shit," I said, remembering my night time stroll to his back porch without notice.

"You're moving in here, too," Vigil told Ryker. "Somehow those fuckers knew Dasia was with us—that means they know about Pia."

"We're not staying here," Ryker muttered.

"Then Greed gets your guest room until this shit is sorted out. Stone?" Vigil turned toward him beside me. "Want to make sure Warden's okay with Ryker stealing his employee?"

"Shouldn't be a problem. Haven't had any big security jobs since the Burtonelli case."

"You and Giada want to stay here?"

"Fuck no," Stone said. "Devil has my place buttoned up like a goddamn penitentiary. We're good."

"Sully can move in here, too, and we'll take turns having two men guard the gate house and man the security system. Pull in Hammer and Crow—those fuckers know how to fight."

Everyone agreed with nods, and Vigil slapped his desk again. "This meeting is fucking adjourned. Let's eat. I'm fucking starved."

19

DASIA

The men came out, a boisterous bunch except for Ricky who stumbled back up the stairs he must have come down earlier.

"Night, night, sleeping beauty!" Greed hollered his way—and got the bird in response. "Grumpy fucker needs to get laid."

"Telling me to go get busy?" Tina asked him, tapping a red fingernail against his cut.

"Fuck no." Greed clasped a hand on her thigh, keeping her close. "You keep that sweet ass right there and keep rubbing against my dick."

Giada made a gagging noise, and I burst into laughter as Pia's face turned beet red.

The men sprawled at one of the tables behind us, and Pia slid off her stool, grabbing the plates and forks. "Foods cold," she said, "but I'll heat it up if you want—"

"Don't bother," Vigil told her while Giada grabbed what was left of the bacon and I gathered up the juice and cups. "I need some goddamn food *now*."

While they ate, I tried Stacey again—went straight to voicemail. Adrian caught my eye, and I shook my head, my stomach churning.

The men scarfed down the food, and Pia, Giada, and I ended up on laps once they finished. Ryker eyed Adrian for a solid minute after tugging me close against his front, but didn't say a word about his hold on me.

One look at my smile, and Ryker heaved a sigh, turning away.

I laid my head on Adrian's shoulder while everyone chatted. "Did you send it?" I asked quietly.

"Yeah, baby."

I let out a heavy breath I hadn't even realized I'd been holding while taking in the group around the table. Had I found my family? Had I found my place, or would this, too, be ripped from me?

"Have you heard from Stacey yet?"

"No."

He huffed a heavy breath but squeezed my ass.

"We're going to be staying here at the club until the ring is taken down."

"Here?" I sat up, glancing around the huge room with its silent sound system, pool tables, and well-loved dart boards against the far wall. Almost empty—for now—but I'd seen how packed and loud the club could get. At least I'd grown used to the underlying stench of stale cigarette smoke and beer that seemed to be baked into the walls and chairs.

"There's a few rooms upstairs," he said, searching my face. "Nothing fancy, but secure as hell. Nothing and no one gets past the front gate without permission. I've got a full security system set up. Cameras in every corner."

"Every corner?" I asked, popping an eyebrow up.

He chuckled and squeezed my ass again, the curve of his lower lip sending a warm tingle through me. "Not in every corner, no. There's privacy upstairs if that's what you're wondering."

"Good."

"Why?" His eyes twinkled. "Planning on having your wicked way with me?"

"The other way around, nerd boy."

"You did not just call me that."

I laughed and threw my arms around his neck,

seeing only him, losing myself in his narrowed gaze. "Nerd boy," I whispered.

"Pussy cat..." he murmured back, sending a riot of butterflies to flight in my stomach.

"You're hot as fuck. Those dreamy eyes, that sensual mouth ... your rock hard body." I pretended to shiver even though he already had me going.

He groaned and shifted me on his lap, making me aware of the thickness growing against my thigh.

I cocked a smirk of my own. "Something wrong?"

"Something needs some lovin' is more like it."

I laughed and pecked his lips.

Someone cleared their throat, and I turned around again. Everyone sat watching us. Warmth rushed to my cheeks. "What?"

Vigil glanced at Ryker who stared at Adrian.

"What?" I asked again, and Ryker let out a grumbled curse or two.

Vigil chuckled, drawing his glare. "Don't say a fucking word," Ryker grunted at Vigil.

"Told you he was a changed man," Pia told the table with a dazzling smile, both dimples flashing.

"I could still rip a fucker's throat to shreds with my bare hands," Ryker muttered, peering down at his calloused palms.

While I knew he didn't like touching people, I

didn't doubt the sincerity of his words—and I felt safer for it.

———

Pia and Ryker left, Greed on their heels. They had refused to stay at the club, so Vigil ordered Greed stay with them in the event any of the Russians came looking for me at their house.

Stone and Giada moseyed out a little after them, leaving the two of us with Vigil who worked on like his fifth or so cup of coffee. Tina had disappeared not long after the men had sat down to eat. Probably snuck up to visit the grumpy Ricky that Greed had said needed to get laid.

I pulled out my cell while Adrian and Vigil talked quietly, mostly guesstimating how long until the shit hit the fan and the mafia had a run in with the FBI.

"Stacey still hasn't returned my call or texts," I said, glancing up from the cell that had zero notifications. "Do you think you can work your magic and somehow check on her? I'd call her parents, but I don't know their number."

"Sure thing, pussy cat." Adrian set me on my feet

and laced his fingers through mine. "She on social media?"

"She's a social media *hussie*, but keeps her profiles private or I'd check on her myself," I said, sitting at one of the two chairs in front of Vigil's desk. "Ryker recommended my staying offline, so I don't even have any apps downloaded on my new cell."

Lips pressed tight, Devil stared at his screen, his fingers flying over the keys. "What does she go by?"

"Her real name..." I pointed as her avatar popped up on her favorite site. "That's her."

Devil pulled her profile up and scrolled down.

Selfies galore—some lower in her timeline included me.

"Oh." He paused, tipping his head to the side to take in one of Stacey and me at the ocean in our bikinis. "Goddamn."

I fake-slapped his arm. "Seriously?"

He laughed and scrolled back toward the top. "Nothing recent," he murmured. "Last post was two days ago."

My heartbeat stuttered, and I leaned forward as though getting closer would help me see something that wasn't there, my throat tightening. "She never goes a day without posting at least once."

Vigil cursed quietly, and I lifted my head to find

him behind his desk when I hadn't even realized he'd come into his office.

He peered at Adrian, his brow slightly furrowed, his pale blue eyes cold enough to send a shiver over me. "See if she's missing, Devil."

Oh God. I gulped, my eyes burning. Pulling my feet up onto the chair and wrapping my arms around my knees, I turned my focus back on Adrian's laptop.

The first headline to pop up caught my breath and sent tears rolling down my cheeks.

Stacey had been reported missing two days earlier.

Another site brought up a video clip of her parents in front of microphones, begging people to call if they knew anything, stating how much of a sweet girl she was, for whoever had taken her to please let her go.

I bit the inside of my lip, but a sob escaped.

"Come here, baby." Adrian pulled me into my arms, his lips on my forehead, and I burrowed against him, clinging to his shirt.

The video clip continued to play.

Stacey had last been seen walking home from school, but none of the local businesses had caught anything on their security cameras. The police had canvassed the neighborhood, but no one's video door bells showed any evidence of a kidnapping, either.

It's like she'd just disappeared into thin air.

Adrian read through another news article that wondered if she'd run off, but I knew my friend. She had a great home life, got along great with both parents—there would be no reason she would just take off.

No. I knew the truth, and exhaustion kept me like a limp noodle in Adrian's arms as guilt ate at my mind. My only friend—I should have known they'd go to her while looking for me. I should have freaking figured that out and warned her.

20

DEVIL

I wanted to carry Dasia upstairs, but she insisted on walking. Her shoulders slumped, she moved into the small room we would call home for as long as it took the FBI to get their shit together.

She slumped onto the queen-sized bed's edge and laid back while I set my laptop onto the used chest of drawers by the door. At least the rooms above the club had been outfitted with small three-quarter bathrooms. Fucking tiny, but they got the job done.

If we wanted food, though, we'd have to head downstairs.

I'd sent Sully off to get all of Dasia's things from Ryker's, but didn't expect him back for at least an hour, so we had some time to chill and process what we'd learned.

I knelt at Dasia's feet and pulled her boots off, expecting she experienced guilt over not thinking to warn her friend. Her stooped shoulders had said it all. "Scoot up there and rest," I said, standing to peer down at her.

She looked up at me, her blue eyes full of pain, auburn eyelashes still wet from the tears she'd soaked my shirt with. "I don't want to rest, Adrian." A shaking hand lifted toward me, and my dick twitched at the invitation. "Make it all go away for a while," she whispered. "Please."

Well, fuck.

I studied her as energetic silence grew between us. How much did she want? How far did she need me to take her in order for her mind to find release?

"Do you trust me?" I asked, my voice rasped at the thought of what I hoped for.

"Yes," she replied without hesitation, still holding out her hand toward me.

I wanted to dive right the fuck in, but something else needed to be said, understood, before I took things any further.

"The thing about being a submissive most people don't understand, is that they control what does and doesn't happen." I peered into her eyes, her slightly furrowed brow letting me know she followed. Her hand dropped to her lap. "You say no, everything stops. Do you trust me to listen to your words—your body's responses, even, if you don't tell me you're not comfortable?"

"So ... you're not *really* in control."

I smirked. "You have all the power here, Dasia. Understand?"

She nodded.

I unbuckled my belt and slid it slowly from its loops.

"Still trust me?" I asked, holding it up.

"You won't hurt me."

"Never."

Dasia nodded, heat growing in her steady gaze even though the pain lingered beyond. "Then give me what I need."

"Take off your clothes, pussy cat," I murmured, my dick fucking swollen and leaking at the green light. "Bare your body to me so I can set your mind free."

And claim your soul.

Keeping that bit to myself, I stood and watched, my entire body tensing as she sat and pulled her shirt off overhead. A flick to the back of her bra spilled her tits free, and she tossed both items to the floor. A wiggle while shimmying down her jeans and panties set those girls swaying, and my mouth watered for a taste—maybe even a few harder nibbles to push her limits on the no pain thing.

Once naked, she laid back, reaching for me again.

"Hands overhead. Grasp the headboard." My dick led the way as I rounded the bed. "I'm going to bind your wrists, okay?"

She nodded, her focus set on my face, no trace of fear in her eyes. "I trust you," she murmured, starting a rush of adrenaline I hadn't ever felt before.

Every brush of my fingers against her wrists and hands seemed to settle Dasia, and until I tied her tight with the leather belt, her lips parted, the pulse in her neck slightly elevated.

"Okay?" I asked again, thrilled to find zero trace of anxiety lining her face.

"Yes." Her smile wobbled, but I trusted her word —and her blown out pupils.

"I'd love to blindfold you, but I won't. This time." I kicked off my boots. "I want you to see who's bound you. Who's touching you. I want you to stay with me, Dasia."

She rubbed her lips together and nodded, her

focus dropping to my dick as I shoved my jeans off. "I will. Promise." Her soft whisper of submission welled pre-cum to my tip.

I grasped my base and slid upward, rubbing my palm over the beaded moisture and slid back down. "Pull your knees up and plant those cute feet on the bed by your ass ... yeah, like that."

She spread her thighs wide, the bare pink petals of her pussy opening for me.

My mouth watered as I crawled between her legs, sliding my hands beneath her ass. Her puckered hole contracted as I slid my thumb over it with a gentle stroke.

Some day.

I leaned in and licked with the flat of my tongue from ass to clit, and she lifted her hips with me as I flicked over her sleepy bud. So fucking sweet and tangy. Another lick earned me a sigh and a coating of arousal over my tongue.

"I could eat this pussy for hours," I said with a groan before diving in for more, every swirl and dip of my tongue over her leaking hole filling my ears with moans and eventually whimpers.

"Do you like my mouth on you, pussy cat?"

"Mmm."

I nipped her swelling labia. "Words."

"Yes."

"Yes, what?"

"I like it when you eat me out."

Fuck.

My dick oozed, smearing on the bedspread beneath my grinding hips. I dipped lower to rim her ass with my tongue, and she didn't shy away.

"Adrian..."

I rubbed my thumb over her hole, gently pressing but not breaching. "Yes, pussy cat?"

"I need you." She peered down over her heaving chest, her pulse throbbing in her neck, a sheen of sweat on her flushed cheeks, the tug she put on my belt shooting an ache through my damn balls. "Please."

My dick sure as fuck needed her.

"Soon, baby." I latched my lips around her clit and slid two fingers deep inside her dripping core.

"Oh." She bit her lip, head tossed back and eyelids closing as she arched, yanking on her restraints. "Oh."

Slow and gentle, I fucked her with my fingers, teasing her hard nub with the tip of my tongue until she panted, tears leaking down her cheeks.

I backed off to yank open the bed stand drawer,

grabbing one of the dozens of condom packets shoved in there for club use.

"Don't need it," Dasia said, breathless, her hair and eyes wild as I sat back on my haunches "I've got an IUD—"

I planked and shoved in with one thrust, knowing I didn't carry any shit to dirty my girl.

"Ah!" Dasia arched beneath me, the fucking clamp of her pussy milking me with her instantaneous orgasm damn near busting my nuts.

I took her mouth, swallowing her cries, thrusting hard and fast, banging the headboard—probably fucking denting the wall, but I didn't give a fuck. I couldn't get close enough. Deep enough.

She squirmed and gasped beneath me, coming down from her climax. "More."

Fuck.

I pulled out abruptly and grabbed hold of her hips, flipping her onto her knees. "Ass up," I growled.

She stretched out, arching her back like a cat in heat, and I pressed back in until my drawn up balls rested against the sticky mess of her cum oozing around my shaft.

Goddamn heaven wrapped up in one red-headed, blue-eyed beauty of a girl who gave herself willingly...

"Dasia," her name left my lips like a goddamn prayer—fucking supplication on my soul, and I bit down on my lower lip while savoring every slow flex of my ass, burying me—dragging me back out—that sweet pussy sucking me back in.

Pure, fucking torture. Slick and hot. Tight as fuck.

Dasia clutched at the headboard around my cinched belt, her head to the side and eyes closed. She panted through parted lips I wanted to bite and lick. Running my hands up her arched spine, I followed along with my torso, pressing my chest against her back until she flattened onto the mattress beneath me.

"Keep your legs together," I whispered haggardly in her ear. "Make that pussy extra tight. Fuck." I ground in, my pelvis pressing tight against her plump ass. "So perfect—so good."

I grasped her chin and turned her face enough I could take her lips, my other hand snaking beneath her belly. Her sweet breath stole mine, capturing me up in her perfection. Losing myself in her, I gave over to the emotion rising in my chest, allowed it to have its way. That fucking rush ... that high of emotion nearly drowned me.

Sliding my fingers alongside her clit, I rubbed them back and forth, every nudge of my hips grinding her pussy against my hand.

"Need you to come around me," I groaned against her mouth. "Take me over, baby. Please."

Her breath caught, and she stiffened, another sweet cry filling my mouth as wetness rushed from her to coat my dick and hand.

Her name groaned from deep inside my chest as my climax slammed into me, every spurt through my dick stealing another piece of my heart and giving it to her to hold. For however long she would have me—I hoped for fucking forever.

Emptied, I kept my weight on my elbows, my lips gentle on hers. Along her jaw, down her neck.

She shuddered beneath me and let out a heavy sigh, a soft smile curving her lips.

Mission accomplished.

21

DASIA

Every muscle in my body turned to liquid, and I sank into the bed, Adrian's warmth against my back, his mouth trailing over my face and neck with gentle brushes of soft lips.

I drank in the affection, the feeling of being important—needed—by someone for the first time in my life. While my first climax had come from one hell of a deep thrust, a harsh fucking, the second welled up inside because of his gentleness, his slow glides and grinds that had taken me higher even than the first.

He'd made love to me. There was no other word for it.

And I fucking loved it. Couldn't wait to do it again. And again.

Sighing, I smiled wider, not giving a single shit over the fact our cum dripped onto the bed beneath us. His cock still buried deep inside me, but began to soften with every heartbeat.

"Stay here," Adrian whispered against my ear before backing off me.

A rush of wetness slipped from me as he slid himself free, and my smile faded over the emptiness, the coolness of the air over my sweat-dampened back. Shivers slid down my spine.

He unhooked the belt from around my wrists, and I fully melted with another sigh.

Water ran in the bathroom, and the bed dipped a minute later, just the nearness of him staving off the sudden loneliness.

"Roll over, baby."

Groaning, I forced myself to do as told, and he spread my thighs, gently wiping our cum from me.

"So pretty and pink," he murmured with the last swipe before leaning down to place a kiss on the top of my bare pubis.

He tossed the rag aside, pulled back the comforter, rolled me onto the sheets while I let out a soft giggle, then climbed in alongside me and pulled the blankets clear over our heads, shutting out the light from the room's single window.

Warm, strong arms tugged me to my side, pressing me chest to chest and nose to nose with him.

My smile returned as he let out a heavy exhale, the sweetness of licorice still hinted in his breath.

"Never letting you go, pussy cat."

"Good." I snuggled against him, the heat of his body almost too much in our dark cocoon, but the comfort of his arms, the protection I felt —perfection.

"Sleep." He swiped his lips over mine in a kiss so tender, so loving, my eyes stung.

I gladly gave into that command, every inch of me wrapped up in Adrian, the devil Viper.

I woke sometime later to his hand between my thighs, his mouth closing over one of my nipples, and the comforter kicked to the bottom of the bed. My body came alive at the heat closing over me and the feathered touch of his fingertips.

"Damn," I moaned, grabbing hold of the hair on top of his head, holding tight. Arousal swelled inside me, quickly slickening me for his wandering fingers. I lifted my hips toward him, my mouth quickly drying as he slid a single digit deep inside me, twisting to rub in a spot that curled my toes. "More," I whispered and wet my lower lip.

He rolled and slid deep inside me with one slow flex of his sexy ass beneath my heels, stilling once buried where he damn well belonged. Amber eyes, still half-closed from sleep peered down at me as he gathered me in his arms.

"Enjoy your nap?" he asked, his tone raspy and sexy as hell while dragging his length out of me again.

"Mmm." I pulled him forward with my legs, gasped as he slid back in, hitting my cervix. "This is better, though."

He chuckled and nipped my chin, and I closed my eyes, giving myself over completely, whole-heartedly to his loving.

"Can we do this forever?" I asked on a sigh, gone on Adrian—the warmth of his skin, the hard muscle pressing against my front, and the softness of his lips.

"We have all the time in the world," he murmured against my neck.

"How long, really?"

Without losing rhythm of his slow fucking in and out of me, he lifted enough to peer into my eyes again. "It'll take them a few days to get a case together and get the warrants they want."

"Days." I smiled and grasped his hair, pulling

him back down toward me and my mouth that needed another taste of him "Sounds good to me."

———

An insistent beeping pulled my eyelids up, and I noted the lack of light outside the window. Turning, I found Adrian gone, his cell beeping from the bed stand.

I lifted up onto an elbow, gaze flicking toward the open bathroom door.

No Adrian.

Blowing out a breath, I sank back again, rubbing the sleep from my eyes. He'd probably gone downstairs for food. God knew I could use something to refill the energy we'd used up staying in bed all day.

A steady throb between my thighs let me know we'd gone at it probably one too many times, but just the memory of having him inside me made me want him again, damn my soreness.

Sighing, I pulled myself from bed, tugged on my t-shirt, and stumbling bow-legged, made my way into the bathroom.

I came out five minutes later, teeth and hair brushed, to find Adrian sitting on the bed's edge, cell in hand, his brow furrowed while reading.

The news clips from earlier slammed back into my mind, damn near stealing my breath. "Any news on Stacey?"

"Nothing." He clipped the word short, but more like something bothered him than mere anger over the fact.

"Everything alright?" I asked, climbing into the bed behind him, settling on my knees close to his side.

"Gram left me a message—said some lawyer is looking for me."

"She say what for?" I asked, peering over his shoulder at his cell.

He'd pulled up a lawyer's website.

"They're going after him."

I studied his profile—the furrowed brow, the muscled jaw flexing as he swiped over the screen— baffled to why a lawyer would call his Gram. I hadn't met her. How would a lawyer have found him if they'd sent everything anonymously through to the FBI. "Ivan, you mean?"

"No. The priest."

Priest ... oh shit. Everything clicked into place in my brain.

"*The* priest?" I asked, watching him closely.

"Yeah."

I waited, deciding to not interrupt his thoughts on what he'd learned.

"Someone came forward to press charges," he finally said, swiping his phone's screen off, "and this lawyer wants to put the fucker away once and for all. Wants me to testify."

He turned toward me, and the vulnerability written across his face tugged on every single one of my heart's strings.

"Will you do it?" I asked quietly, running my fingers along the edge of his white t-shirt he hadn't tucked into his jeans.

"Bet your delicious ass I will." He grabbed me up in his arms and planted a kiss on my lips, and I couldn't keep from laughing at the sudden turn of emotion.

"That fucker's gonna pay, isn't he?" I said between kisses.

Adrian pulled back, the devil glinting in his eyes. "We'll make sure he does."

I lifted an eyebrow. "Care to explain?"

"Club business." One last smooch, and he hopped up, smacking my ass when I teetered on my knees. "As much as I want that ass, you better cover it. Sully ordered pizza and it'll be here soon."

"Can I have a beer?"

He snorted while grabbing my jeans off the floor and tossed them to me. "No."

I pouted, and he tipped his head to the side, focus on my mouth. "What?" I asked, all innocent and wide-eyed while poking my lip out even farther.

He adjusted the bulge in his jeans, his gaze narrowing. "You."

"Me, what?"

"Get your damn clothes on, pussy cat. I'm hungry —for food."

"And my ass?"

He licked his lips, slow and sensually, heating me from the inside out in a flash. "Dessert."

Well.

Heart thrumming and butterflies fluttering, I did as told, ready for a taste of the forbidden. After pizza, of course.

22

DEVIL

Never in a fucking million years did I expect I'd be given a chance to help put that fucker behind bars. Sully knew all about that pile of shit part of my life, and we discussed it over our pizza, Ricky even dragging his ass down after I'd smashed my fist on his door until he'd answered.

He sat broody as hell, nursing a beer after only a single slice while Dasia flitted around the kitchen area, cleaning up and grabbing us some cold beers.

We ended up hanging out in the club afterward with its handful of pledges and a few other brothers in for their week night drinks and darts. In a corner, I hunkered over my laptop, pulling up too many fucking memories for my liking. While only one newspaper and station reported on the accusations against the priest, I knew I wasn't going to pass up the opportunity of helping to end him.

I'd buried the hurt years ago, put it in the fucking slammer deep inside my soul, refusing to sift through the contents of what had turned me off from the church.

The news, though, had popped that fucking lock, and it all came back, ugly as fuck. Gut-twisting as fuck.

Dasia's hand on my thigh helped keep me grounded while looking at his ugly mug again. The warmth of her pressing against my side kept me focused on the *now* of the moment rather than the past.

Within an hour, I listed out those men I expected he'd either paid off or called in favors from in order to keep his ass out of jail the first time around. A few I already had shit on since Vigil made it my job to keep abreast of crooked dealings concerning those in authority in our area.

The judge who let him off—a friend of Giada's father. The second, one of our state's two senators. A handful of lawyers and another group in law enforcement, too. Add in one of the church's biggest supporters, a Midas-like businessman from Boston, and I couldn't help but grimly grin over the money I would wring out of their sorry asses.

"What are you doing?" Dasia asked against my ear, and the club came back to my senses. Too-loud music. The two brothers, Hammer and Crow, still playing darts puffing away on cigs and clouding the room.

Ricky had left, as had Sully for the guard house.

I glanced back at my screen, shutting it down for the night, every bit of information I'd glanced over tucked into my head for safe keeping—and later evaluation.

"Doing what I do best." I closed my laptop down, looking for a distraction.

"What?" Dasia asked as my attention went to her face and completely stalled out.

"You're the best distraction in the goddamn world," I told her, serious as fuck. "Not sure if that's a good thing or not."

Her slow smile pinged me like a damn dart right in the heart. "You get so caught up in that damn computer—I'm thinking I'm a *good* distraction."

I groaned and pulled her onto my lap, my favorite place for her. "Yeah." Smoothing back her hair from her makeup-less face, I grinned. "You are."

She wrapped her arms around my neck and

leaned close, her lips a breath from mine. "Thank you."

"For?"

"Helping me. Caring for me. Just being you." Her soft lips brushed against mine, twitching my dick. "No one has ever made me feel this way, Adrian." She pulled back, her fingers still in my hair, her eyes serious.

"How's that?" I asked, lacing my fingers behind her back.

"Like I have worth. Like I'm important beyond something to lust after while I strip."

I considered joking about the type of lust I feel when she's taking her clothes off, but the sincerity of her tone and on her face kept me on the same level.

"I'd sell my soul to the devil himself to keep you safe."

She studied my eyes. "You really mean that, don't you?"

"Bet your juicy ass I do."

Pink flushed her cheeks and she bit on her lower lip. "About that..."

"Yeah?" One of my eyebrows shot up.

"You have any ropes around the club?" She glanced away, the pink turning redder by the second.

"I was thinking I wouldn't mind a little more kink exploration."

My dick swelled. "How far are you willing to go, pussy cat?" I murmured, leaning in to nip her lower lip.

A shiver rippled over her as her pupils expanded. "I-I don't know, but I'm all for finding out exactly how sick I am."

Sick. I snorted.

"Nothing sick about it, baby. If my pussy cat wants to play, I've got all night to make her feel good. Your wish is my fucking command."

"In that case, I'll see you upstairs." Dasia climbed off me, and I adjusted my dick while watching her saunter toward the stairs.

She caught more than my attention, and I shot a glare at the prospects who gaped after her ass, darts and beers in hand.

"Don't swallow your goddamn tongues!" I yelled at them, deciding to grin rather than threaten them to within an inch of their lives like Ryker or Warden would do.

Nah. That pussy cat was all mine, and having men salivating after her only swelled my fucking chest with pride. Add in the excitement of putting my past to rest for fucking good, and I felt on top of the world.

Laptop under one arm, I made my way into the kitchen and the stairs to the small basement area where we kept our stock of guns, ammo, and supplies in the event the zombie apocalypse ever happened. There had to be rope down there.

Time to tie up my girl for real and see how far she let me take her before tapping out.

DASIA

My heart pounded as I sat on the bed's edge, waiting for Adrian. While I hadn't felt an ounce of fear or been bashed in the head with memories over his tying my wrists to the headboard, I wondered if I might feel differently being completely bound.

At his mercy.

That part got my insides thrumming, keeping my panties in a constant state of wetness.

I wanted to be spread out, tied up, unable to move while he took what he wanted. I'd never given myself willingly, I'd only been taken, but with Adrian, I wanted it.

My heart longed for it. Submitting fully, I had a

feeling, would give me a sense of empowerment. Fulfilling his desire for us...

A shiver raised goosebumps along my arms, and I kicked off my shoes, so damn ready I couldn't stand it. He liked bondage, and I was pretty sure I did, too. Match made in heaven? Sick kink, a little broken, but like he'd said, we could be that together.

I eyed the bags Sully had dropped off earlier, and I chewed on the inside of my lip while considering putting on something different than my jeans and t-shirt. He'd prefer me naked, I knew.

My hands shaking, I stripped bare, tossing my clothes and boots into the corner. I tried to lay all sexy on the bed, fluffing my hair out, propping up on an elbow—and felt like a fool. Spread eagle, awaiting his ropes? I didn't feel much better in that position, staring at the ceiling, either.

He wanted my submission, and although I knew he enjoyed my sassiness, perhaps offering him myself *fully* would be best.

I sat up and knelt in the middle of the bed, head lowered and hands on my lap. My pulse thrummed and belly danced full of butterflies as my ears strained to make out footfalls in the hallway.

Steady breathing in and out calmed my racing

nerves and centered my mind. Adrian had given me so much, had gone way beyond what anyone ever had for me that I wanted to give him what he wanted.

I want this. I want him.

The door creaked slightly, sending a shot of adrenaline through me, but I kept my head down, hair cascading around my body.

Adrian's groaned curse brought a smile to my lips. "Goddamn," he said a bit louder, shutting the door quietly behind him. His boots thunked to the floor, but I kept still, eyes shutting to better focus on his moving around the room.

Clothing rustled and soft footsteps sounded closer.

"You're a fucking vision, Dasia, offering yourself to me like this." Haggard, his voice hinted at what I did to him.

Wetness eased from between my thighs, and I pressed them tight together as a deep throb beat in time with my heart.

The scent of him drifted past my nose, and I breathed him in, the butterflies in my belly taking flight once more.

"You're sure about this?" he asked, his voice low and to my right.

"Yes," I whispered.

"If it's too much—at any time—you tell me, and everything stops, remember?"

I nodded.

"Words, Dasia."

"I understand."

"Good. Lift your hands out in front of you, fingers clasped."

My arms trembled, but I did as told. At the first brush of something along the inside of my wrist and upward, I shivered.

"It's just the rope."

I blew out a breath and nodded again, keeping my eyes closed as he familiarized me with the feel of the rope he planned to bind me with.

Adrian ran the length up my arm and back down before wrapping it around my wrists, binding them together. He continued loops and tucked up my forearms, tying them tight up to my elbows.

"Okay, baby?"

"Mmm." *More than okay...*

He wound another around my chest like a harness, the soft caresses of his fingers along the sides of my girls keeping me grounded. One flick of his thumb over my hardened nipple, and I moaned, my head tipping back.

"Look how beautiful you are."

My eyes opened on command, and my shoulders relaxed, my lips parting on a quick exhale. A light brown rope wrapped and looped up my arms, tight but not uncomfortable in the least, the slight abrasive texture of the rope seeming to make the rest of my body's skin sensitive. My already big breasts plumped from the wrapped rope above and below.

"Lay back."

I lifted my focus to Adrian's face—and lost my breath.

Such longing filled his gaze, those bedroom eyes drinking me in, studying my face as though making sure I was really okay. He'd stripped down to his jeans, popping the button to tease me with that happy trail my tongue had the sudden urge to lick. The tip of his straining dick peeked out, and I *did* lick my lower lip.

He chuckled. "Lay back, pussy cat."

Letting out a huff, I scooted onto my back and raised my arms, expecting the bit of rope he'd left hanging from my wrists was intended for the headboard.

As expected, he rounded the bed, and I tipped my head back to watch his face as he tied me tight. God, the curve of his lips drove me insane. I wanted his mouth on me.

"Adrian..."

One corner of his lip curled as he glanced down at me. "Patience. We're not nearly done."

Another huff left me, and he grabbed up two more lengths of rope before climbing onto the bed between my legs. He lifted one foot, kissing my toes, before setting it back on the bed, heel against my ass.

I closed my eyes again, losing myself in the sound of his breath, the slight scratch of the rope as he bound my ankle to my thigh and wound upward toward my knee. Every slight brush of his skin, every murmur of approval over my relaxing beneath his touch set me more at ease even though my body burned for him.

He tied the other leg and moved to my side. My head seemed light—floating on air. My leg moved easily with his as he pulled it higher, stretching me wide open, knee almost to my chest.

Tugs on the harness...

Another murmur of approval...

He moved around to my other side, and I realized through the buzzing in my brain that he'd tied my leg to the harness. I couldn't move my leg.

Panic should have set in as he lifted my other leg, leaving me open and vulnerable to the extreme, but wetness dripped from my body onto the bed. I felt no shame, only desperate need.

Lips parted, I panted softly, ready for whatever he wished.

Complete trust.

Complete surrender.

I lost touch with reality, the pleasant buzz in my brain shutting off sound, every nerve ending on my skin alive and tingling.

Waiting.

His palm slid up over my shin, dipped to my belly, which shivered beneath his light touch. Upward, he stroked around my breasts, his heightened breaths reaching through the rush in my ears.

"So beautiful," he murmured, grasping both of my nipples in his fingers.

I moaned, lifting my chest toward him, needing more.

So much more.

Warmth and wetness covered my pussy—Adrian's mouth—and I gasped, the swelling of my climax imminent. One flick over my clit, and I cried out, coming against his tongue, the wet sounds of his lapping and sucking on my labia like an erotic movie in my mind.

"Goddamn, I could eat you out all fucking night

long." He licked from asshole to clit. "So creamy." Another lick. "Fuck."

He disappeared, but I kept my peace, trembling and coming down from the intense waves that had washed over me, taking me to another dimension where nothing but him existed.

A drawer sounded—a cap.

My body tensed at what that meant, but I breathed out, forcing myself to relax. I wanted this first with him.

A cool, slick finger slid down through my pussy lips. "Your pussy is swollen and red."

The roughness of his tone licked across my skin, tightening my nipples into aching buds as his finger pressed into me. "Are you sore, baby?"

"A-A little," I whispered the truth even though I would have taken him into my pussy if that's what he wanted.

Slick and gentle, he fucked his finger into me twice more before slipping it out and down, coating my asshole with my cum and lube.

"Relax," he cooed, one hand soothing my inner thigh. Gentle pressure, and he slid in slightly, making me furrow my brow at the strange sensation of having the tip of his finger in my ass. "Okay?"

"Mmm." I nodded, eyes still clenched shut.

He pushed in farther but retreated before I could squirm. Another rimming, and he slid back in, deeper, filling me until his knuckles rested against my ass.

Different, but hardly unpleasant.

Twice, he pulled out and pushed back in, his other hand lowering to my clit. A few flicks on my sensitive nub, and his finger moving in and out of my ass took on a whole different feel, beyond different—it felt fucking *good*.

My lips parted as my body heated, and I found myself pushing toward his hand.

"Like that, baby?" he whispered, and I murmured my approval again.

He pressed a second finger in, taking his time to work in deep, the slight scissoring of his fingers creating a delicious burn that caused my pussy to pulse.

My legs began to shake, and I tugged against my arm restraints, desperate to touch him. Grab his hair and pull him against me.

"Please ... Adrian, please."

"Hmm?" He added a third finger, and my eyelids shot open at the sting. He held my stare, lust darkening his eyes and swelling another climax to life deep inside me with every deep stroke of his fingers.

I lost myself in his eyes, as though our souls connected, bound tightly to one another—I needed more.

Whimpers escaped me, my hands grasping at air, my legs trembling in their restraints.

"I got you, baby," he murmured, pulling his fingers from me, leaving me empty enough a dry sob wracked through me. "Got you." He wiped his hand on a rag and stretched over me, one hand on his swollen, glistening dick, working his length, the other planted on the bed beside my knee.

He pressed the head of his cock against my stinging hole. "Let me in..." A gentle nudge slipped him past the ring of muscle he'd loosened, but fuck...

Too big.

Too much.

I panted, whimpers escaping with every exhale as he pushed in another inch. "Oh God." I grit my teeth, my eyelids slamming shut once more. Sting. Fullness. Fuck, he was too damn big.

He planted his other hand beside me, took my mouth in a gentle kiss, his tongue sweeping along my lips, tasting. Teasing. I let him in, moaning at the sweetness of his breath, the softness of his mouth. Lush. Damn delicious. Nibbles and licks took my mind off the massive cock head shoved a few inches up my ass, and the sting faded as he feasted on my mouth.

A flex of his hips pushed him deeper, and I moaned at the havoc coming to life inside me.

My pussy ached and dripped as he backed off and slid back in. Deeper. Another withdraw and another gentle thrust slid him in so damn far I lost my breath.

He groaned against my mouth, his kiss turning hungrier. Heady and almost frantic—but he kept from fucking into me like an animal.

"Dasia..." His body trembled above me, and he sat up, tearing his mouth from mine. "Look at me."

Panting, my mind in a vortex of need, I lifted my eyelids and fought to focus on his face.

Jaw clenched tight, he peered down at me. Sweat glistened on his tensed shoulders, and I realized he fought for control.

"I can take it," I whispered, that feeling of being in control rushing through me. "Give it to me."

He shoved in fully, arching my back off the bed.

"Adrian!"

He grasped my thighs. "Sorry, baby," he growled, his control snapping, hips thrusting in and out. "Gonna tear this ass apart—fill you with my cum."

Relaxing wasn't an option as he plowed into me

over and over, but I found I needed more, the mixing of slight pain and absolute torturous pleasure every rough thrust spiraled through me, throwing me towards oblivion.

Adrian slid two fingers inside my pussy, his thumb on my clit—and I came with a shriek, wetness rushing from me, my pussy pulsing, my entire body convulsing in my restraints.

"Yeah ... fuck." His fingers worked me fast, rubbing deep inside me as he shoved deep into my ass, my cum squirting over his hand and cock. "Squeeze my dick, pussy cat, take it all."

He grunted and slammed in deep, his cock swelling. Wet heat shot inside me, his cock jerking, every slight thrust of his hips as erratic as his grunts and groans.

I went lax before he did, gasping for breath, my lips dry as fuck, every muscle in my body trembling.

Good and truly wrecked.

Best. Feeling. Ever.

24

DEVIL

Dasia lay lax and pliant as I cut her free and carried her into the bathroom where I'd gotten the shower going. I held her tight against my front as she melted against me, her cheek on my chest, her arms in a light hold around my waist.

We stood sideways beneath the spray, the water hitting the back of her head and my right side. A shuddering sigh—at least the fifth since I'd fucked her ass—escaped her lips.

I hadn't checked in with her nearly as much as was probably appropriate, but the lack of tension on her face the entire time I'd trussed her up let me know all I needed to.

Dasia trusted me. And she definitely got off on being tied up. I hadn't planned on taking her ass, but with her spread open like a goddamn buffet, her pussy red from our fucking earlier in the day, and that untried rosebud...

She hadn't tapped out at one probing finger. Her pussy had oozed cream as I added a second, and the haze of lust in her eyes when I'd stretched her with three...

My kinky little pussy cat. She'd taken it all, every goddamn inch of me into her tight body.

"Goddamn, you're something else," I groaned, squeezing her tight. "You okay?"

"Fuck, yeah." A light laugh shook her in my arms, and she tipped her head back. Flushed face. Strands of red hair plastered to her cheek from the shower's spray. Eyes bright yet satiated.

"So, do you still think getting tied up is sick?" I had to ask, my own lips curling upwards.

"No. It's hot as fuck." She leaned up, and I lowered my head, giving her my mouth. "I want to do it again," she said against my lips before sliding her tongue between them.

Goddamn, this woman...

I pulled her up into my arms, and she wrapped her legs around me.

Never enough.

Fucking *never*.

For three days, we stayed holed up in our room, only going downstairs to shove food in our faces before escaping back upstairs. Without rings in the ceiling like I had plans to install at home, I couldn't string Dasia up, but we made do. I wrapped her with decorative patterns, that when taken off, the rope left gorgeous as fuck indents in her pale skin.

I tied her tight, immobile, legs spread or sometimes pressed tight together but pussy and asshole available for the taking. She'd had a taste of my dick up her ass, and she fucking loved it. My kinky, little pussy cat couldn't get enough.

Twice, Ricky pounded on our door telling us to calm the fuck down and shut the hell up so he could sleep.

I felt for the guy, but not enough I invited him to join in like we'd done a time or two with club whores.

Nope. Dasia was all mine—her lush body, her quick mind, and her soft heart. She'd claimed to be broken, but she was goddamn perfect in every way.

Perfect for me.

We were perfect for each other.

My cell rang, dragging my exhausted ass out of

sleep. Morning light hinted around the blinds as I grabbed my phone off the bed stand, knocking the bottle of lube beside it onto the floor.

I recognized the lawyer's number, but didn't answer in time.

Laying on my back, still grasping my cell, I waited for the ding of the voicemail to sound.

Dasia peered at me through sleepy eyes—fucking beautiful without a stitch of makeup.

I leaned over and kissed her lips. "Morning."

"Mmm."

My cell dinged, and I pulled up the voicemail transcript.

"What is it?" Dasia asked, propping up onto her elbow.

"Deposition is scheduled in three days."

"For the priest?"

"Yeah." I tossed my cell aside, for the first time ever excited to meet with a lawyer for something legal. "Gonna bury his ass." I pushed my girl onto her back, both of us laughing, and within seconds, buried myself deep in her wet heat.

25

DASIA

Adrian was gone most of the day to give his deposition down in Boston, so to combat boredom, I started cleaning. It began in the kitchen when I went down for coffee after he left and found a mess left from the brothers who'd partied the night before—too loud, the damn men kept me awake long into the night.

Adrian and I had found things to combat the sleeplessness, though, mainly me tied spread eagle like a buffet, and oh, how he had feasted.

Sully and two other bleary-eyed brothers sat at the kitchen's table nursing mugs when I walked in.

"Morning," Sully muttered into his cup, lacking the usual jollity in his voice I was used to.

"Hey." I grabbed a mug and poured what they'd

left while the other dirty blond-headed guys who looked like brothers grumbled a greeting.

I made a second pot while sipping the dregs from the first pot. My stomach rumbled, so I started opening cabinets to see what I could find. They didn't offer much.

Pulling open the fridge revealed a box of left-over pizza with Greed's name scribbled in black marker across the top. The "Property of" had me snickering.

These men and their claiming.

It was kinda hot—I wouldn't argue. I'd noticed a few of the old ladies had that very thing tattooed on their skin along with their man's name. I grew warm thinking about having Devil's name inked on me. With his love of my ass, I knew I'd get a nice script along my lower back for him to stare at while he pounded me from behind.

Warmth grew between my thighs, and grumbling internally about his not being back to the club for a few hours at least, I pulled out a dozen eggs that sat alongside the pizza box.

"You boys hungry?" I asked without turning, grabbing the tub of butter and a loaf of bread.

"Shit, yeah," Sully muttered. "You gonna hook us up, Kitty?"

Kitty. I huffed a bit of laughter. "That gonna be my nickname?"

"Can't call you pussy cat like Devil does," Sully said. "So, Kitty it is. Better than DeeDee, too. Sexier." He chuckled.

Well. I grinned while dragging out a pan and spatula. *I have a nickname.* Warmth of a different sort flooded through me, a feeling of belonging, that feeling of what I expected family must be like.

Fifteen minutes later, we all held egg sandwiches —three with ketchup slathered inside, mine without.

I found myself snickering again as Sully and the other two moaned and groaned over every mouthful. You'd think they never had a home cooked meal even if it was a simple one.

I worked with Sully, a goofy Irishman with dark hair and equally dark eyes that twinkled even when his lips weren't smirking. The other two, brothers by blood, I learned, Hammer and Crow, short for crowbar, had their own construction company. They'd built Adrian's house a few years earlier and had been hanging since Vigil moved us in almost a week earlier.

While cleaning up after the boys, I considered Adrian's home and wondered over what future we might have. I went from scrubbing dishes to wiping down the counters, and moved to cleaning out the fridge, my mind flying from one thing to the next, getting out restless energy.

I lived at the club for free, so why not do my part to help out?

Adrian had told me one of the club whores—not Tina—was paid to clean the place once a week, but she sure as shit didn't do a good job. Once finished with the fridge and taking out the trash bag of moldy shit I'd found inside it, I stood, hands on hips, taking in the kitchen as a whole.

While the floor was a decent tile, a darker tint hinted at the most travelled areas. The cabinet faces had finger prints around the knobs and splatters across some of the lower ones. Add in the old beer spills, sticky beneath my slippers, and I couldn't fucking stand it.

Lips in a thin line, I yanked open the cabinet doors beneath the sink and found what I needed— rubber gloves, a small bucket, rags, and a spray bottle of cleaner.

Two long as hell hours later, that fucking room sparkled and smelled fresh as a baby's ass—a clean one.

Satisfied and smiling, I made my way back to the

main area. The bar snagged my attention, but I'd had enough of wet scrubbing. The entire room needed a good dusting and sweeping.

Sully watched from one of the couches on the far wall, his dark eyes full of mirth. "If Devil doesn't keep you, I'm available for the taking. Just sayin'."

I smirked. "Where's the vacuum?"

He pointed toward a door. Behind it sat a janitor's closet of sorts, the shelves stocked with extra toilet paper, paper towels, and other cleaning supplies. I got to work while Sully, Hammer, and Crow bullshitted. Turned out, all three were my guards for the day, and another two sat out in the guard house watching over the security cameras Adrian and Warden had installed.

Hammer and Crow were more on the quiet side, both cute as hell with wide shoulders and greenish eyes, but they didn't compare to my Devil.

Mine.

Yeah. I liked that thought. Maybe I could get him to tattoo "Property of Kitty" across his hard pecs.

Vigil, Pia, and Greed showed up with a pile of groceries not long after I started vacuuming, and Pia helped me clean while Vigil and Sully headed out to the shop to work. Vigil's suggestion I spend the rest of my work day doing what I'd been doing all morning kept me put, rather than out in the shop I'd been ignoring since moving into the club, and also kept my mind occupied from missing Adrian too much. I ended up wiping down the baseboard and all the chairs and tables, disinfecting the stale cigarette scent from every surface possible while Pia made a huge pot of chili to simmer on the shiny stove top.

I took my sweaty ass to our room once finished, and stood beneath the hot spray, washing off the ick from my hours of work, missing Adrian like mad. We'd spent days on end without a break from one another, and I liked it. Maybe too much.

The bathroom door opened, and I welcomed my man into my arms, my world completely right again.

"How'd it go?" I asked as he tugged me tight against his chest, melting my body against his hard warmth.

He grinned, those sexy as hell lips curving to the point my stomach flipped full of butterflies. "That fucker is going down. They've got so much shit on him, he doesn't stand a chance of paying his way out of it this time."

I leaned up on my tiptoes and he met my mouth halfway, both of us greedy. With a groan, he yanked me up into his arms, and I settled my legs around his waist, the cold tile pressing against my back.

One thrust seated him deep inside me, settling my world *entirely* right. I'd found my forever home with Adrian, I just hoped nothing in our future would threaten it.

He grasped my ass cheeks and buried his face in my neck, teeth nipping over my sensitive skin while dragging his hard cock out of my clenching walls and shoving back in.

"Fucking perfect," he growled against my neck, his fingers bruising my flesh, "Fucking missed you."

"Missed you more," I managed to gasp out between pants.

"Fuck, baby…" He ground his pelvis against me, and I fell apart in his arms, shaking and crying out with my climax. Two more grunts, and he came with me, his hot cum like a brand against my womb.

"Devil!" A fist pounded on the bathroom door, and I seized up with a quick shriek.

"The fuck, Ricky?" Adrian hollered, his face falling into a scowl.

"News just broke! Fucking take down of the goddamn century!"

Adrian caught my gaze, and we stared, both still

gasping for breath and coming down from our climax high.

"Cut your fuck session short and get your ass downstairs!"

Adrian grinned and gave me a quick peck on the lips. "Ready to go see if our plan worked?"

"He *said* takedown of the century."

"I'm thinking freedom, pussy cat." One more peck, and he backed out, leaving me dripping.

A quick scrub, and we tossed on clothes, hurrying downstairs to see what sort of future I had ahead of me.

26

DEVIL

Ricky had the main room's TV on NECN when we got downstairs, both of our hair still soaked. At least Dasia had wrapped hers up in a sexy as hell messy bun. Mine just plastered to my forehead, but I brushed it back, not giving two shits what it looked like.

The newscaster laid it all out—what they knew so far, anyway. Dozens of men had been taken into custody, some being named and labeled. The head of the Russian mob in New England. Fucking Martínez, the head of the Martínez cartel. They even had an image of him in handcuffs where he'd been nabbed at Logan Airport while coming in from South America on his private jet.

I fucking cheered at that one.

They showed clips from the harbor—and young women being led out of containers.

Dasia gasped and stepped closer toward the TV, and I followed after, wrapping my arms around her waist and setting my chin on her shoulder. She chewed on her lower lip.

"I don't see her," she whispered, lacing her fingers through mine and squeezing tight. "I don't see her."

Stacey. Shit.

The newscaster went onto something else, and I kissed Dasia's cheek. "Be right back." I sprinted upstairs, grabbed my laptop, and hurried back to my woman who stood right where I'd left her.

I pulled her along toward Vigil's office, glancing at Ryker who had come over from the shop at the same time we'd gotten downstairs. He dipped his head at me, Pia tucked against his side, teary-eyed, although hope filled her smile.

They followed on our heels while the rest of the brothers hung in the main room, their focus still on the TV.

While the club as a whole didn't know all the details, they knew the basics of what had happened to my girl and also knew we'd taken measures to see the fuckers behind bars. They just didn't know the lawless extent I'd gone to ensure my pussy cat could walk around free from fear.

I booted up in my usual spot in front of Vigil's desk, and set to work hacking into the security system I needed access to. Slipping in the back door was too damn easy, but same as always, I thanked the IT gods for idiots who didn't know how to fire-wall against sneaky fucks like me.

"Dasia." I motioned her over from the couch, patting my lap. She sat facing my screen, and I scrolled through files around her, recalling when the newscaster said the busts had begun. I clicked on the right timeline and started the feed, keeping it on fast forward until the action began.

FBI agents and SWAT teams swarmed the harbor, and I clicked through different camera feeds, finding what I needed.

A few tweaks cleared up the grainy images enough the girls being led out into the light were clearer beyond what the media had managed to get their hands on.

Dasia leaned forward, her hands on Vigil's desk as she studied each and every one.

"Stacey," she breathed her friend's name, her palm slamming over her mouth. A sob ripped from her lips.

I reached around her to pause the feed. "That her?"

Dasia nodded, tears rolling down her cheeks.

"Thank fuck," Ryker muttered, and I glanced over to find him holding Pia in his arms. She, too, cried, fat tears slipping down her face.

Only time would tell what we'd truly managed to accomplish, but I held onto hope enough of the fuckers had been taken down that Dasia could live without fear for her life.

———

Vigil came into the club along with Warden and Stone, and we all sat around the club eating chili with shredded cheddar, chives, and sour cream, and homemade corn bread slathered in butter, while the TV continued with coverage on the confirmed sex slave operation take down.

Klingon called Vigil, letting him know over a dozen Vegas fuckers involved in the same mob had been taken into custody, bringing the total number to thirty-two.

Alexi Dvornikov, aka Ivan the sex slave ring leader, the fucker I wanted to end, had also been arrested along with his two goons, Dasia confirmed upon seeing their faces. The tears had given way to a healthy, happy glint in her eye, and she packed away the food for the first time since I'd met her.

She laughed. Joked. Her eyes sparkled with life, fucking beautiful, and my heart ached to tell her how much she had filled my life to the fucking brim.

I carried her upstairs before everyone else left for the night, Sully, Hammer, and Crow staying, too.

I set my girl on the edge of the bed and cradled her face while kneeling between her legs.

"Thank you," she whispered, her eyes welling even though the joy there stole my breath.

"I'd do it all over again—fifty fucking times, Dasia."

She laughed lightly. "I don't mean all the illegal stuff—I'm talking about healing me."

I lifted an eyebrow, my focus dropping to her plump lips. "How so?"

"Showing me the difference between sickness and healthy kink. For showing me the difference between sick obsession and overwhelming desire that can be rewarding as hell."

We stared at one another, her smile slowly fading, the energy growing to a crackling level between us. My dick swelled, priming with pre-cum to slicken my glide inside her tight pussy—my pussy. My woman.

"No one has ever made me feel this way," she whispered. "No one has cared the way you do. No one in my life has ever made me feel loved." Her breath caught, and she snapped her lips closed, that word ringing between us.

My slow smirk swelled her pupils—the girl couldn't hide her lust for my lips. "I *do* love you," I said.

Her gaze ripped off my mouth to my eyes, her gaze piercing—searching.

"I'm not lying, pussy cat," I told her, my voice serious as fuck even though I still grinned. "You're the fucking light of my life, cheesy as that sounds. You're the best reason a man could have for opening his eyes in the morning and think about while jacking off."

She laughed, and I pressed my lips to hers, cutting her off.

"Fucking love you, Dasia," I whispered against the soft cushion of her mouth. "Now, tomorrow—and forever. You're my number one."

The wetness of her tears slid between our lips, and I pushed her back onto the bed, standing to rip off my shirt.

"You're more than just a set of thighs to rut between," I said, shoving down my jeans as she shimmied out of her leggings. "Don't ever fucking doubt that, pussy cat."

Dasia reached for me, and I slid home, my forehead pressed to hers, our breaths mingling between us as I held still ... waiting to see how she wanted it.

"I love you too, Adrian," she whispered, and my chest seized up tight as fuck while I dragged my dick back out to the head. She squeezed her thighs tight around me. "But I need more right now than making love."

"Call me Devil," I told her with a growl and slammed back in, pulling a shriek from her lips.

Fuck, yeah. She wanted it rough, she could have the devil inside.

She fucking owned him, made him her bitch.

27

DASIA

A week after the big take down, I finally got to hear Stacey's voice. She hadn't been raped—thank God, but it had been Ivan and his goons who'd grabbed her off the sidewalk while she'd been walking home from school that Friday. And yes, I'd mentioned Pia to her that day on the phone—and she'd known Pia had moved to the north shore to be with her motorcycle man.

Learning she'd gotten two black eyes and one smashed finger to get that information out of her made me feel like absolute shit, but also gave me that same sense of belonging, as though I had a true friend in my corner.

Stacey had spent time in a basement, same as

me, and had been tossed into the container at the harbor less than twenty-four hours prior to the arrests and the women's rescue.

Two weeks later, she'd healed and felt well enough to drive up to Topsfield to hang with me at Adrian's house, my forever home, for a couple days.

Adrian felt it was safe enough for us to head out for a girl's day since there were no known Russian goons or Martínez cartel members on the loose. Not a single one cuffed that day had been given bail, and although three of the Russians were wanted in their home country, the US refused to ship them home without standing trial for their crimes against our citizens.

We got our nails done, hit up a bakery for sugar and caffeine, then on a whim, I decided to stop at the tattoo shop—and not tell my man.

"So he's it, huh?" Stacey asked, chin in her palm as she leaned on the arm of the chair beside me while the burn continued along my lower back.

"Without question," I answered, never more sure of something in my life.

"Eighteen is kinda young to settle down," she muttered, her lips downturned. "You've got your whole life ahead of you—and you obviously don't have that PTSD shit I've got going on. You're nuts for settling for him."

"I'm not settling, Stacey," I said with a frown of my own. "He's the best thing that's ever happened to me. Seriously. The day we left the club for his place, he swept me up into my arms to carry me over his threshold like some goddamn gentleman of old. He claimed if I wanted a picket fence, he'd have one put in. If I wanted his walk-in closet, it was mine." I huffed a snort in memory of the next line. "He even told me if I wanted kids, he'd give me ten—whatever I wanted."

"You told him hell no."

"Got that right." Stacey knew I had no wish to bring a child into the world when I didn't even know where I'd come from. "He doesn't want any either, but the fact he was willing to cave for my sake..."

A resigned smile lifted my best friend's lips. "He's so gone on you."

I laughed, remembering the way she'd looked at him looking at me that morning over the late breakfast I'd made for her arrival. "He is, isn't he?"

"You're so lucky." Stacey sighed and sat back, the furrow between her brows appearing again. "I'm so fucked up in the head," she muttered. "I can't imagine allowing a man to touch me ever again. And that pain with the pleasure thing? Fuck, no. I'm so over that shit."

I reached out a hand and clasped hers. "Give it time," I told her, my voice close to breaking. "I'm ten times as fucked up as you, and I found the one man willing to sacrifice everything he has for my wellbeing."

She nodded, but my heart continued to ache for her.

We stayed up until all hours of the night watching Marvel movies, Adrian leaving us for our bed and crashing long before either Stacey or I fell asleep on the sectional to dreams of my man Thor and Captain America's ass.

I'd managed to keep my tattoo a secret by sleeping downstairs, and also avoided alone time with Adrian throughout the next day to keep him from seeing it before I could take the plastic covering off.

While he'd stolen a few kisses and handfuls of my ass, I held him off for over twenty-four hours, the longest we'd gone without fucking in some way or another.

When Stacey left at sundown the next night, I promised to tell her all the juicy details of Adrian's seeing my tattoo for the first time. I should have prepared myself a bit because even though I'd grown damp at the thought of what he might do, I didn't expect the rough toss over the back of the couch and him slamming deep inside my body before I could breathe.

One rough fuck later, he laid me on my belly in the middle of our bed and kissed every inch of my tattoo, giving me the softer side of his devilish nature. My nerd boy made sweet love to me, leaving me in a puddle of liquid bones, sweat, and sticky cum.

I felt like a million bucks with his declarations of love ringing in my ears.

We settled into a routine while awaiting two trials—the priest and the mob men.

I played the dutiful home maker even though I worked at the shop three days a week for Vigil. We continued with our karate classes, and Adrian couldn't help but cop a feel every time we sparred.

Jack never looked my way again, and Lini smirked every time she caught Adrian grabbing my ass.

He had me show off my tattoo to the entire club after us both having a few too many drinks one Friday night while the place rocked.

I ended up dancing with Giada, Tina, and a

couple of other women while the prego girls sat on their men's laps. Giada and I ground against one another, earning hoots and hollers, but a new song started up where the last ended, the thumping bass one I'd danced on stage to.

Eyes on Adrian, I moved to the routine I'd created to stuff my G-string full of bills—but I kept my clothes in place, loving how not one trace of discomfort or PTSD smacked me in the face. The devil filled his eyes, his smirk a heady sight I couldn't tear my focus from. Everything faded but him. The amber glow of lust in his eyes, the sensual curve of his lips, the tension in his shoulders—and the bulge between his spread thighs he didn't bother trying to hide.

I ended up on his lap, grinding away like a few of the club whores did to other brothers, but not one lick of embarrassment rose from my actions. I was simply Devil's pussy cat wanting his attention, rubbing against him in the way I liked in order to get what I wanted.

I found myself tossed over his shoulder, hair dangling almost to the ground, his palm firm on my ass while striding toward the stairs. Laughing, I lifted my head to find the clubhouse cheering him on. My face finally flushed, and I waved, blowing a kiss to

Ryker who lifted his tonic our way—without a trace of a scowl on his face.

My family.

Adrian tossed me onto the bed we'd spent a couple of weeks in, and I soaked in the feeling of *home.*

28

DEVIL

I placed my right hand on the Holy Bible and swore to tell the truth and nothing but the truth, so help me God. The fact I went by Devil wasn't lost on me while reciting those words in a goddamn court of law.

I'd never been more ready to uncover the fucker's sins to the public like I'd been kept from doing while a kid and make him pay. I was the third such man to take a stand to testify for the prosecutor, but it was the two younger boys and the images they had captured with a cell phone that sealed the priest's fate.

Their devious means of catching the fucker after months of abuse tickled my damn funny bone. While the jury sat in deliberation, I clasped both their shoulders and told them to come find me when they turned eighteen. Their eyes gleamed when I told them I rode with the Vipers and promised to sponsor them if they ever wanted to prospect.

The jury took all of an hour to come to their conclusion, and as the gavel fell, sentencing the cocksucker who'd almost ruined my existence to spend the rest of his in prison. I felt as if the last piece of my life's puzzle had finally slipped into place.

Clutching Dasia's hand tightly in mine, we left the court house—free and clear for whatever the fuck fate had in store for us.

———

"He's going to the maximum security prison over in Shirley," Vigil told me as I walked into his office the next afternoon.

He'd called us in for church, but I left my pussy cat out at the bar with the other old ladies. While Warden wasn't an officer, he tended to sit in as Vigil's enforcer.

Stone, Vigil, and Ricky had already beaten me there, and I wasn't one bit sorry for being late. I'd gotten a little ... tied up with my pussy cat and the rings I'd had installed in our bedroom's ceiling. My dick twitched at the memory of seeing her strung up in my ropes even though I'd blown my load all over her tits and face.

Clearing my throat, I sat in my usual sat across from Vigil and met his pale-eyed stare. "Got anyone in there we know?"

His smirk would send a shiver through a lesser man. "Darling."

I huffed a laugh. "You're shitting me."

"Nope. He got transferred over there last month."

"Well, damn." I couldn't keep my grin contained. "He's gonna make that priest his bitch."

"Goddamn right."

Darling was a mean mother fucker Vigil had known as kids, and he'd been in the slammer for over ten years, doing hard time for a double murder. Even though the fuckers deserved to have their limbs lopped off for what they'd done to Darling's mom, the jury he'd stood before didn't feel the same enough to keep him from doing time.

He'd been a Viper prospect, but had gone off on his own quest for revenge, and the cops found him before his soon-to-be brothers could help him out, before our cleaners could cover his ass.

He and Vigil had kept in close contact over the

years, and he'd been crucial in helping us get shit from other inmates we could use against those who'd tossed them in there.

Knowing the priest would soon be on his knees—probably toothless from fists—and sucking down a dick he'd have shoved up his own ass, fulfilled that need for physical revenge I hadn't been able to dish out personally. Sick satisfaction coursed through me, and I glanced over to find Ryker watching me.

I nodded his way, finally understanding why he enjoyed ripping out throats so damn much.

"And what about that Ivan fuck?" Ryker asked. "Any news on him?"

"He's the one spilling all the mob's secrets in exchange for leniency."

"Pussy," Ricky muttered, slouched in his chair and broody as fuck—what else was new.

"He won't see the light of day until he's in his forties or so," I said with a shrug, "but I'll find his ass once he's out. No fucking witness protection can hide him from me. I'll bloody my hands one day. No fucking doubt."

"And with the Russian mafia gone from our area and the Martínez cartel splintered to shit with him being found guilty already..." A wicked grin curled

Vigil's lips. "Seems we might have ourselves a bit of quiet around here for a change."

"Good," Ricky muttered.

"Maybe we'll get lucky, little brother," Vigil said, still grinning. "All these fuckers found their old ladies—maybe a set of twins, young juicy ones, will show up at the gate for us next." He grabbed between his thighs and sat back, stroking himself in front of us without a fucking care of what we thought. "Don't know about you, but the whores just aren't doing it for me anymore. Need some fresh blood, I'm thinking. Someone who doesn't know how to suck dick like a pro. Gagging and tears—all that shit. Fuck, yeah."

Stone shook his head, as did Warden. I sat unmoved, unbothered by our president's lack of filter.

"Goddamnit." Vigil dropped his hold on his dick and smashed his palm onto his desk. "Get the fuck outta here—and Ricky, send in Tina, will ya? I can get her to gag sometimes if I catch her off guard."

Biting back my chuckle, I headed out into the club behind Ryker, the too-loud country music some schmuck had put on whining from the overhead speakers.

Dasia sat with her back to me, chatting with the

ladies, but as if she could sense my presence, she straightened and turned before I moved three feet in her direction. Her smile fucking dazzled, one I would never grow tired of seeing. Those lips, those unpainted blue eyes—all for me, and all mine.

I pressed up against her back, my mouth finding her neck. She smelled like spring flowers—my heaven, my fucking property. My teeth grazed her soft skin, and goosebumps rose along her arms as she went lax in my arms, head tipping to the side in complete surrender to whatever I wished.

My kinky pussy cat.

Grasping her chin, I turned her face toward me for a nice, long taste of her mouth. "Want to hang here," I whispered, "or head home so I can string you up from our bedroom ceiling?"

She shivered and wet her lower lip. "Take me home, Adrian."

"The name's Devil," I said with a wink and grabbed her hand, pulling her toward the door.

THE END

———

ABOUT THE AUTHOR

Lynn Burke is a full-time mother, voracious gardener, and International Bestselling Author of hot romance books. A country bumpkin turned Bay Stater, she enjoys her chowdah and Dunkin Donuts when not trying to escape the reality of city life.

ALSO BY LYNN BURKE

Blood Born Series

Bonds of Worship Series

Darkest Desires Series

Dark Leopards MC

Devil's Outlaws MC

Elite Escort Series

Fallen Gliders MC

Found by Fate Series

Midnight Sun Series

Missing Link Series

Risso Family Series

Sandy Ridge Series

Vicious Vipers MC

Standalone Titles:

Abel's Obsession

Divulging Secrets

Healing Storms

In Between

The Playboy Bachelor

www.ingramcontent.com/pod-product-compliance
Lightning Source LLC
Chambersburg PA
CBHW071248190726
48292CB00007B/2454